Every inch of Rafael's tall, lean, muscle-packed frame oozed sex— every hollow and plane of his dark face. Maggie's eyes drifted from the full curve of his sensual upper lip to his hooded glittering gaze, and her level of anxiety went off the scale.

'You've never had a one-night stand, have you?'

Maggie considered lying, but decided it was doubtful she could pull it off. 'Not as such...' she conceded reluctantly.

He leaned into her close, very close, but not touching. 'But you came with me. What were you thinking of...?'

Kim Lawrence lives on a farm in rural Anglesey. She runs two miles daily and finds this an excellent opportunity to unwind and seek inspiration for her writing! It also helps her keep up with her husband, two active sons, and the various stray animals which have adopted them. Always a fanatical consumer of fiction, she is now equally enthusiastic about writing. She loves a happy ending!

UNDER THE SPANIARD'S LOCK AND KEY

BY
KIM LAWRENCE

First published in Great Britain 2010
Harlequin Mills & Boon Limited,
Eton House, 18-24 Paradise Road, Richmond, Surrey TW9 1SR

© Kim Lawrence 2010

ISBN: 978 0 263 21355 3

Harlequin Mills & Boon policy is to use papers that are natural, renewable and recyclable products and made from wood grown in sustainable forests. The logging and manufacturing process conform to the legal environmental regulations of the country of origin.

Printed and bound in Great Britain
by CPI Antony Rowe, Chippenham, Wiltshire

UNDER THE SPANIARD'S LOCK AND KEY

CHAPTER ONE

SUSAN Ward manoeuvred herself down the ramp into the kitchen, her daughter and husband protectively shadowing her progress.

Propping her crutches against the chair her husband pulled out, Susan lowered herself into her seat, ignoring her nearest and dearest as they hovered anxiously.

Maggie, watching the procedure apprehensively, released a relieved sigh when her mum was safely seated. 'You're getting pretty good on those things, Mum,' she observed, privately concerned that she was also far too ambitious. It was lucky her dad was now retired from his job on the oil rigs so was around to keep an eye on things when she wasn't.

It had been three months since the experimental surgery, but to see her mum, who had been confined to a wheelchair for the last eighteen years, on her feet even for short periods still gave Maggie a thrill.

And now, if things went according to plan, in a couple of months she would no longer need the chair or even the crutches.

Susan dismissed the comment and turned her frowning regard on her daughter, who took a seat opposite. 'Never mind that, how are *you* feeling? *Really* feeling,' she added, holding up her hand in anticipation of her daughter's reply.

'She looks exhausted, doesn't she, John?' She appealed to her husband for support.

John Ward's warm glance swept his daughter's pale face, touching the warm dark ebony curls that clustered around her heart-shaped face. 'She looks beautiful.'

Oh, well, Maggie reflected, at least I have got one fan even if he is my dad. 'Thank you, though according to you I was beautiful when I was twenty pounds too heavy, had teenage acne and braces,' she reminded him.

'Don't change the subject, Maggie,' her mother said sternly.

'I told you, I'm fine, Mum,' she replied, pasting a determinedly cheerful smile on her face to illustrate the level of her fineness.

She had perfected the 'I'm fine' smile a long time ago, because no matter how bad her day had been Maggie had always been pretty sure growing up that her mum's had been worse.

This conviction dated from the day when her dad had returned home from the hospital with her baby brother and no Mum—she had been four at the time.

Her other brother Ben, at the noisy toddler stage, had run around the room while John Ward sat with baby Sam in his arms and explained to Maggie that Mum would not be coming home yet and when she did Maggie would have to be a big girl and help her because Mum was not well.

Maggie had only vaguely understood the explanation of what was wrong with her mother, but she had known it was bad because her big strong dad didn't cry.

The tears had scared her and made her feel sick inside. She had begged him to stop crying, and promised that if he did she would never *ever* be a bad girl.

Of course she had not been able to keep that promise, but

the determination that had been born that day to protect her mum and stop her dad crying had never left her.

Compared with what her mum had coped with, a broken engagement and a cancelled wedding faded into insignificance.

'Seriously, I am fine,' Maggie promised in response to the sceptical looks directed her way as she anchored her heavy dark hair at the nape of her neck with one hand and accepted the mug of coffee her father passed her. 'I'm just sorry about messing everyone about this way,' she added, her brow furrowing as she tried to calculate how much her parents had already laid out on the wedding.

It was easier to address the practicalities of the situation than think about what an idiot she had been. 'All that money,' she fretted.

'Forget the money,' her father said firmly. 'That's not important—' He broke off mid sentence as the door opened to let in a cold gust of air and two young men in muddy rugby kit.

They ignored their sister, grunted in the direction of their father and mother before heading for the fridge.

'Glass, Sam,' Susan said out of habit as her younger son raised a carton of milk to his lips.

He lowered the carton and said, 'We lost, if anyone's interested.'

His older and slightly more intuitive brother nudged him with his elbow and removed the pad he was holding to his own cut lip. 'They're not interested, Sam. So what's up, guys?'

Maggie got to her feet. Telling her parents had been bad enough—they at least, bless them, had not asked any awkward questions even though she knew they were dying to. She could not, however, rely on her brothers to be similarly restrained. 'Nothing. That lip could do with a stitch,' she added, casting an expert eye over her brother's mouth.

Ben rolled his eyes and, taking the carton from his brother, took a swig of milk before subjecting his sister to an equally critical narrow eyed stare. 'Sure. You *always* look like death warmed up.'

'I've just worked a ten-night stretch in a busy casualty department,' Maggie reminded him.

'So?' Ben retorted, looking unimpressed. 'Nothing new there—you always work crazy hours. You have to be certifiably insane to be a nurse.'

'Thanks.' Maggie's mouth twisted into a grim little smile.

Simon had called her the *perfect nurse.* The recollection sent her stomach muscles into tight unpleasant spasm, though, to be totally accurate, apparently Simon had been quoting his mother, the possessive Mrs Greer, whom Maggie had found to be manipulative and very overprotective of her only child, when he said this.

She resisted the temptation to cover her ears as snippets of that conversation drifted through her mind.

'Obviously you won't work when we are married. You can help out with my constituency work, and the social engagements.'

'I like my work,' she had replied, wondering how Simon would take the news she had no intention of giving up work.

'Of course you do, darling. Mother has always said you are the perfect nurse and when she moves in—'

Maggie had been unable to hide her horror. 'Your mother is going to live with us?'

Simon had looked annoyed by the interruption, giving a thin lipped smile. 'Of course.'

He had made it sound as if it were a done deal, and why not? she thought with a grimace of self-disgust. She had always gone along meekly with what he said.

'Did you get any injuries from the train derailment I saw on the telly, Mags?'

Maggie dragged her wandering thoughts back to the present and responded to the ghoulish enquiry from Sam with an absent nod of her head.

'That explains why she looks so wrecked,' Sam observed.

Ben shook his head. 'No, it's not work...' His eyes widened. 'Are you pregnant?'

The colour flew to Maggie's cheeks, and Susan Ward looked uncomfortable, making it obvious that this had been her first thought too.

'*Ben!*' his father warned.

'No, it's OK, Dad,' Maggie said, placing her hand on her dad's shoulder. 'It's not a secret.' She took a deep breath. 'If you must know the wedding is off.'

Sam closed the fridge with his elbow and let out a silent whistle. 'So no more slimy Simon!'

'Simon is not...' Maggie stopped. Actually he was. She suddenly felt pretty stupid that her little brother had recognised the characteristic and she hadn't.

She had wasted four years of her life on Simon, which might have been acceptable if she had been desperately in love with him, but Maggie now knew she hadn't been.

Maybe she was one of those people that couldn't fall in love? A depressing thought but a definite possibility; she had certainly never experienced the sort of blind, intense passion her friends spoke of.

'Do you have to send back the presents? There's a coffee maker that's much better than the one we have—'

Sam's brother cut across him. 'Did he dump you? Or...God, had he been cheating on you?' The idea drew a chortle of laughter from his brother. 'I didn't think he had it in him.'

'Simon did not sleep with anyone.' Not even with me, Maggie thought, swallowing the bubble of hysteria in her throat.

'Well, what did he do, then?'

Maggie's eyes fell as she hesitated. For the first time in her life she felt awkward bringing up the topic of her adoption.

She had never had any hang-ups at all about being adopted, no yearning secret or otherwise to find her natural mother—it had never even occurred to her that Simon had any concerns.

Though concern was clearly an understatement considering the lengths he had gone to to trace her birth mother. Thinking ahead, he had called it; anticipating future problems, he had explained with a self-congratulatory smile.

Maggie closed her eyes and could hear him calling her birth mother's identity 'a potential skeleton-jumping-out-of-the-cupboard situation' before going on to explain in the same pompous manner that a politician in his position—one with a future—could not be too careful.

'He had a problem with...' She looked at the expectant faces and hesitated again.

Mum and Dad had told her years ago that they would understand if she wanted to contact her birth mother, but Maggie had never believed they could be as all right with the idea as they appeared.

Maggie, who had always been keenly conscious of the crazy guilt thing Mum had about not being able to do the things with her children that able-bodied mums took for granted, had no intention of searching out a mother who was able to enter the mums' race on sports day.

To her mind even thinking about her birth mother felt like a betrayal of the parents who had loved and cared for her, and why contact a stranger who had given her away and risk rejection for a second time?

Would they believe that Simon had made the unilateral decision to search for her birth mother? Or would they think that she had decided they were not enough family for her? Maggie decided there was no point taking a risk.

'It was a lot of little things. We simply decided that we didn't suit. It was all very amicable,' she lied, absently touching the bruised area on her wrist.

'Maggie will talk about it when she's good and ready and you two,' John Ward said sternly, 'have all the sensitivity of a pair of bricks. Your poor sister—'

'Had a lucky escape,' Ben interrupted. 'And don't look at me like that—I'm only saying what everyone else is thinking. Sorry, Maggie, but it's true.'

Susan broke the awkward silence that followed this pronouncement.

'What you need is a holiday.'

Maggie laughed. 'You think I should go on the honeymoon cruise?'

Maggie had no desire to go on the cruise that had been a cause of friction. Though Simon had reluctantly agreed that it might not be proper to take his mother on their Mediterranean honeymoon, he had assured her that next time of course she would go with them; Mother apparently loved cruises.

He hadn't asked Maggie if she enjoyed them.

'Oh, goodness, no, there'd be too many middle-aged people on a cruise,' Susan exclaimed, adding, 'Where did I put those brochures you brought home the other day, John? I think they're on the piano stool. Go get them, Ben.'

'Mum, I can't go on holiday. There's so much to do. I need to cancel the—'

'Your father and I will do that.'

John nodded. 'Of course, and you might as well say yes, Maggie, because your mum will wear you down eventually. She always does,' he added, dropping a kiss on the top of his wife's fair head.

He wasn't wrong. By the time the weekend was over Maggie found she had booked herself on a European coach tour.

Her mum had mixed feelings about her choice.

'But, Maggie, there will be nobody under forty on a coach tour.'

'Mum, I'm not looking for romance.'

'What about fun?'

It was a question that Maggie considered on more than one occasion over the next few weeks.

Maybe, she mused, she ought to put sensible on hold and try spontaneous, though not as spontaneous as her friend Millie had suggested when she heard the news of the broken engagement. Fun was one thing but, as she told Millie, the idea of a casual fling with a stranger did not appeal to her.

She had responded with a mystified shake of her head to Millie's suggestion that she might not have met the right stranger yet.

What Millie didn't get was that she simply wasn't a very *sexual* person.

CHAPTER TWO

RAFAEL worked his way across the room crowded with members of two of the most ancient and powerful families in Spain, brought together to celebrate the baptism of the twin boys who were the result of the marriage that had joined the two dynasties.

His cousin Alfonso, a frown on his face, approached.

Rafael arched a dark brow. 'A problem?'

'I've just been speaking with the manager, Rafe.'

Rafael nodded encouragingly.

His cousin shook his head and said quietly. 'I can't let you pay for this, Rafael.'

'You don't think I'm good for it?'

His cousin laughed. The extent of Rafael's fortune was something that was debated in financial pages and gossip columns alike, but even the most conservative estimates involved a number of noughts that Alfonso, who was not a poor man himself, struggled to get his head around.

Like all the Castenadas family members present, Alfonso was *old* money, though like many of the old families, including his wife's, the Castenadas family were not the power they once had been.

Except Rafael, the family maverick whose massive fortune was not down to inherited wealth.

When Rafael's father died in a sailing accident he did leave his son an ancestral pile and several thousands of acres, but the land that hadn't been sold off had been mortgaged to the hilt and the ancestral pile had been sadly neglected.

The estancia had needed a massive investment of, not just cash, but enthusiasm and expertise to bring it into the twenty-first century.

Rafael had both.

In the last year Rafael-Luis Castenadas had added a news-paper and a hotel chain to his already wide-ranging holdings. It was a long way from the disgrace Alfonso's uncle had always predicted his son would bring to the family name.

'If he was still with us Uncle Felipe would have been proud of all you've achieved.'

Rafael raised a dark slanted brow to a satirical angle. 'You think so?'

Alfonso looked surprised by the question. 'Of course!'

Rafael shrugged, recalling his father describing his career choice as a 'passing phase.'

'All things are, I suppose possible.' All things except his ability to please his father, Rafael mused, unable to recall the *exact* moment he had realised this, but able to recall the sense of release he had got when he'd finally stopped trying.

Following this revelation there had been a short interval when out of sheer perversity he had adopted a lifestyle guaranteed to embarrass his father.

He had rapidly outgrown the rebellion, but he was still paying the price for this youthful self-indulgence, those early colourful bad-boy antics had attracted the attention of the press at the time, and Rafael had never totally shaken that youthful reputation or the interest of the media.

'But surely…' Alfonso protested.

Rafael's lips curved into a sardonic smile.

'My father was an elitist snob—being a Castenadas was his

religion.' How anyone could think an accident of birth made him somehow better than his fellow man had always seemed bizarre to Rafael.

The lack of emotion in the dry delivery, as much as the sentiment, made his cousin stare.

Reading the shock and disapproval Alfonso struggled to hide reminded Rafael that, though he had always got on well with his cousin, who was the epitome of a decent guy, when it came to family pride they were not reading from the same page.

'You will allow me to give my godsons this gift.'

Responding to the charm in Rafael's smile—very few did not—Alfonso grinned back. 'Gift? What were the cases of vintage wine?'

Rafael's arm moved in a dismissive gesture. 'Wine is a good investment and I managed to locate some rare vintages.'

'I'll say, and I'm grateful on the boys' behalf but that's not the point, Rafael.'

'The point is I wish to do this for my godsons. They are, after all, my heirs.'

Alfonso laughed. 'I won't raise their hopes. You're thirty-two, Rafael—I think you might manage an heir or two of your own,' he observed drily.

'I have no interest in marriage.' Why perpetuate a flawed formula?

He was surrounded by failed marriages, unhappy marriages and expensive divorces. If marriage were a horse it would have been put down years ago on compassionate grounds, but it was a product of wishful thinking and people, it seemed, needed dreams.

Rafael was content with reality.

He rarely had a relationship that lasted more than a couple of months, which was as a rule about the time when he started hearing *'we'* a lot. It was also generally around this time he began to find the qualities that had first attracted him to a woman irritating.

He was not waiting to find his soulmate.

'I will leave the domestic bliss to you and Angelina. I do not buy a restaurant if I want a meal and I do not intend to take a wife in order to have sex.'

Alfonso winced and said, 'Nice analogy.'

'I do not have a reputation for niceness,' Rafael reminded him. He did, however, have a reputation for being utterly ruthless and single-minded when he pursued a goal. It was debated whether it was this ruthlessness, his sharp analytical mind or a combination of the two that accounted for his success.

Rafael, not given to introspection, had never attempted to analyse the formula; he did what he did because he liked the challenge—when he stopped enjoying it he would walk away.

An hour later all was still going smoothly—so far, at least. In the days when he'd had to attend every last family event, Rafael had seen far too many that had gone sour to rule out the possibility totally.

It might at least liven the proceedings, he mused, and almost immediately felt ashamed of the selfish sentiment. This day meant a great deal to the proud parents so for their sake he hoped the day stayed boring.

With luck he would not be obliged to see his family until next Christmas.

He put down the drink he had been nursing since he arrived, glanced at his watch and wondered when he could leave without causing offence.

'Have I thanked you for all this?'

He turned at the sound of the voice behind him, the hard light of cynicism that made several of his relatives uncomfortable absent from his eyes as he smiled at Angelina.

It was hard not to smile, not just because his cousin's wife was a beautiful woman—it was more than that. Angelina was the most genuine person he had ever met, she had a warmth that made people around her feel good.

A tall woman, and one blessed with symmetrical features set in a perfectly oval face, a slim, elegant figure and an aura of serenity, his cousin's wife was probably many men's idea of a perfect woman.

Rafael had wondered more than once why he wasn't attracted to her in a sexual way, but he never had been.

'Alfonso has already thanked me.'

She watched the uncomfortable look cross his face and gave him a hug. 'Why do you hate people to know you can be nice?' she wondered.

'I am not nice. I always have an ulterior motive—ask anyone.'

'Yes, you're totally selfish. I can see how much you're enjoying yourself.' She angled a quizzical look at his dark face. 'Wondering when to make your escape?'

There was an answering smile in Rafael's eyes as he asked, 'Should I mention you have baby vomit on your shoulder?'

Angelina carried on smiling, displaying a perfect set of white teeth as the dimple in her chin deepened. 'No, Rafael, you should not.'

The first time he had seen Angelina and Alfonso together it had been obvious even to a cynic like him that they were crazy about each other, and as far as he could see the honeymoon was still on.

Ten years down the line, who knew?

'Motherhood suits you.' He saw the flicker cross her face and knew he had inadvertently dredged up a memory.

'Thank you, Rafael. The twins, it's hard not to think about... It was all so different this time.'

Rafael had no trouble interpreting the disjointed sentence. He watched her swallow and wished he had kept his mouth shut.

He saw her lips quiver and hoped she was not going to start crying. He put a lid on his empathy, a sympathetic word or gesture now would no doubt open the floodgates and he had a major dislike of female tears. 'Why think about it?' he said brusquely.

Rafael's philosophy was if you made a mistake you lived with it. Beating yourself up over it was to his way of thinking a pointless exercise, and an indulgence.

'You're right.'

'If only more people realised that.'

Generally appreciative of his ironic sense of humour, Angelina did not smile.

Her shadowed eyes were trained on the far end of the vaulted hall where her husband, a son balanced expertly on each arm, paused to allow admiring relations to kiss the cherubic cheeks.

'He is such a good father.'

'And you are a good mother, Angelina.'

She shook her head. 'It makes me think...did I do...?' She lifted her troubled brown eyes to Rafael. 'Was it the right thing?'

Rafael had no doubt. 'You did the right thing.'

Rafael had strong feelings about advice: he never requested it and he never gave it.

It was a sound position, it was just a pity that he had forgotten and made an exception for Angelina.

'But I hate lying...'

'Confessing might have made you feel better, but what would it have achieved other than—?'

'Make Alfonso call off the wedding. He would never risk a scandal.'

'Maybe,' Rafael lied. In his mind there was no maybe.

He actually had no doubt at all what the outcome would have been had Angelina found Alfonso and not himself at home the day she had arrived at his cousin's city apartment to confess all.

Would Alfonso have felt sympathy for Angelina, forced to give birth at sixteen to her married lover's child? Yes.

Would he have married her after she had confessed? No.

'You did the right thing, Angelina. Why should you suffer now for a mistake you made when you were little more than a child? You were the victim then—is it fair you be the victim now? Everyone makes mistakes…'

'Alfonso doesn't,' she said wistfully.

Rafael might have said that Alfonso wasn't perfect, but he knew it would be a waste of breath. To his wife he was.

'It doesn't seem right I'm this happy. I wonder if she's happy, my little girl. I wonder sometimes…'

'Better not to,' Rafael advised tersely. 'Why think about what you can't have?' He had wasted many nights wanting his mother back, but he was no longer ten and he knew better.

CHAPTER THREE

MAGGIE WANDERED THROUGH the winding streets just soaking up the atmosphere. She had a whole afternoon to do her own thing before she needed to be back at the hotel for what the tour guide had enthusiastically described as an '*authentic paella experience.*'

Attendance was optional but he'd told her it was highly recommended.

Having paused for a glass of wine at a pavement café, she pulled the map from her shoulder bag. The tour guide had declared the street market a *must* for any visitor to the city in search of authentic Spain and, according to her map, it was really close.

Half an hour later and totally lost in a maze of alleys Maggie decided to admit defeat. With the clock ticking and the tour guide's instruction to be back at the hotel by seven if she planned to join the group for dinner, she finally decided to head straight for the cathedral.

Maggie was just beginning to think that she would miss out on seeing that too when she spotted the distinctive spire of the cathedral directly ahead.

Standing on the pavement, sweat trickling down her back—the day had been hot; the evening was sultry without a breath of breeze to offer relief—she waited for a lull in the steady stream of traffic. It quickly became clear there was none. Not that this seemed to bother other people, who just stepped confidently into the road weaving their way through the traffic to an accompaniment of horns, yells from drivers and rude gestures to the opposite side of the congested road.

Before she could think better of the idea she stepped out.

The security outside the hotel was tight; the media had been kept away, only a couple of approved photographers had been permitted access, though unfortunately Rafael's departure co-incided with their arrival.

'Since when were *you* camera shy, Rafael? I'd heard you are *very* photogenic. I think your face and reputation keep half the scandal rags in business.'

Rafael reacted to his elderly uncle's cackle of laughter with a sardonic smile.

'I suppose I was slightly naive to think that my family at least would give me the benefit of the doubt.' Rafael liked women, he liked sex, but if he had bedded as many beautiful women as the press liked to suggest he doubted he would have the strength to get out of bed.

'You were never naive, Rafael—not even when you were a baby like those two… I remember your baptism like it was yesterday,' his uncle reminisced. 'You bawled your head off all through and your father kept saying, "Elena, do some-thing," and she did, though I doubt if Felipe had an affair in mind.' He angled a look that held more curiosity than apology at his tall great-nephew's face as he added, 'No offence intended.'

The muscles along Rafael's strong jaw tightened, but his expression did not change as he promised, 'None taken.'

'Her mistake was confessing. Honesty is not the best policy, especially when dealing with people like your father. How old were you when he…?'

'Threw her out? Ten.'

Old enough to feel angry and betrayed. An image flashed into his head and he felt nothing as he watched his ten-year-old self begging his mother to take him with her and shouting when she tearfully sobbed she couldn't.

'It was a tragedy she died so young.'

Before he ever had a chance to retract the things he had yelled at her as she left.

Not insensible to the sensitivity of the subject, Fernando slid a glance at Rafael's stony profile before observing, 'There are worse things in life than being considered a sex god.'

'A hard reputation to live up to.'

The comment drew a laugh from the older man. 'Modesty,' he mocked. 'That's not like you, Rafael.'

'You think I need a lesson in humility?' Meekness was to his mind an overrated virtue, he had never turned the other cheek in his life and he wasn't about to start any time soon. In his world displaying any weakness was fatal.

'You care what I think?' Fernando stopped dead, his attention straying across the road. 'Now that is what I call a re- markably good-looking woman...she reminds me of someone...Rafael...?'

It was not hard to identify the object of his relative's ad- miration. She stood poised uncertainly on the edge of the pavement watching for a gap in the heavy traffic that moved through the congested street.

A little above medium height, she had a natural poise and elegance that made her stand out from the crowd even wearing standard-issue faded denims and a loose cotton tee shirt that hinted at the lush curves of her breasts, the natural attribute he suspected had first drawn his reprobate great uncle's atten- tion.

As his glance moved upwards to her face she stepped back- wards as a scooter mounted the pavement. As she lifted a hand to throw the ponytail that had flopped forward over her shoulder her head turned and he saw her face for the first time.

The breath left his body as Rafael froze, feeling as if someone had just landed a punch in his solar plexus.

'Over there…I think she's trying to cross the road. You see her?'

'I see her.'

'Now that is what this party lacked—a few pretty faces to look at.'

'Not pretty,' Rafael contradicted.

His elderly relative looked outraged. 'Not pretty? What is wrong with you? Don't tell me you like your women like sticks. A woman should be soft and—'

'Beautiful,' Rafael corrected, cutting across his great-uncle's list of womanly attributes.

As his brain emerged from its temporary paralysis his eyes remained trained on the slim figure, but it was not the brunette's face or her indisputably womanly figure that held his stunned gaze.

He glanced briefly at his great-uncle, who played the forgetful old man card when it suited him but was anything but; the last thing Rafael needed at this moment was Fernando to realise why the girl looked familiar to him.

He was surprised he hadn't already.

The sooner he got him safely away from this potentially explosive scene, the better.

Rafael dragged his eyes off the brunette. Still aware of her in the periphery of his vision, and aware he was not the only one aware of her—this was a woman accustomed to male attention—he offered his great-uncle a supportive arm, nodding to the driver who held the door open as Fernando took his place in the car.

The car moved off and Rafael was able to focus all his attention on the brunette.

She was obviously heading for the hotel. If she walked in now he could imagine the reaction and there were photographers to record the moment for posterity and every tabloid on the planet!

An illegitimate love child reunited with her mother while the unsuspecting husband and social elite looked on. My God, the girl had to have engineered the moment for maximum embarrassment—not that her motivation or her feelings were what he needed to concentrate on now, he told himself, blocking out this line of speculation.

This was about damage limitation. Let Angelina have this day at least before disaster in the shape of this girl arrived.

He couldn't let her go into the hotel.

So how did he stop her?

He found himself wistfully contemplating a less civilised and much simpler age when he could have simply slung her over his shoulder.

This not being an option, he had to repress his natural instincts and opt for more subtle methods. As he sifted through the possibilities he was very aware that no matter what action he chose, he could not give this situation a happy outcome.

The story had everything: sex, money and a beautiful woman—or in this case two!

If she walked through those doors now he could imagine the reaction to that face and tomorrow's headlines. He couldn't allow it to happen.

Rafael tried to narrow his focus to the here and now. It was a struggle: he had a mind wired to asking why...where; a question mark was a challenge to him.

As he walked towards the road his mind was working fast as he sifted through the possibilities. What was she doing here?

Coincidence did not even make it to the list.

Rafael did not believe in coincidence any more than he

believed in the Easter bunny or the general decency of his fellow man…or in this case woman. He did believe in protecting the people he cared about.

His silver grey eyes narrowed. The brunette, her hair and other things bouncing gently, had begun crossing the road towards the hotel entrance, confirming all his worst suspicions.

He felt something kick low in his stomach—anger, he told himself—as he watched the gentle sway of her hips in the tight jeans she wore.

Of course there were decent and genuinely *good* people—people like Angelina. He liked to think he was not without the odd scruple, but this woman was not one of life's innocents.

It always amazed Rafael how that vulnerable minority managed to get through life with their ideals and their lives intact while most people were out for what they could get regardless of the people they trampled over in their pursuit of whatever ambition drove them.

What was driving Angelina's daughter?

Greed, revenge…possibly a combination?

A child genuinely wishing to discover a parent would hardly choose a public occasion to do so.

Then as he watched she stepped off the pavement. *Dios,* he might not have to worry about scandal—the girl was a traffic statistic waiting to happen!

It was pure luck that she reached his side of the road before disaster struck—or almost. He watched as she jumped in response to the blast of a scooter horn as it whizzed past her, lost her footing and began to fall back into the moving traffic.

CHAPTER FOUR

MAGGIE lifted her head, a smile of gratitude ready to thank the person who had leant a steadying hand and pulled her onto the safety of the pavement.

'Thank you…' The words and the smile died a death as she found herself looking into the lean face of her saviour.

The sound of the traffic retreated somewhere into the recesses of her shell-shocked brain. She was looking into the dark face of the most beautiful man she had ever seen or even imagined.

She was too startled to disguise her reaction. Maggie's gaze travelled in wide-eyed appreciation over his strongly sculpted features.

This was not a face anyone would forget in a hurry.

As a child Maggie remembered wondering what her mum had meant when she spoke of someone's 'beautiful bones.'

He was what she meant.

The genetic gene pool had been very generous to this tall Spaniard, who had been gifted cheekbones sharp enough to cut yourself on, a strong aquiline nose and a firm, angular jaw.

His unlined brow was broad and intelligent and he possessed the most striking eyes she had ever seen—pale icy grey, almost silver, the striking colour intensified by the dark ring around the iris, they were fringed by incredibly long spiky lashes that were as dark as his strongly delineated ebony brows.

But it was his mouth that Maggie couldn't take her eyes off. Was it the hint of cruelty she saw in the sensual curve of his sculpted lips that tugged so strongly at her senses and made the aura he projected so overtly sensual and masculine?

Close your mouth, Maggie, you're drooling.

In an effort to respond to the ironic voice in her head, she gave herself a mental shake.

It didn't help. Her head remained a swirl of impressions and her nerve endings continued to thrum, sending shivers across the surface of her overheated skin.

She'd had too much sun, Maggie decided, shading her eyes as she struggled to find an explanation for being struck dumb and foolish at the same moment—an explanation that did not involve being in the presence of a six-feet-four black-haired Mediterranean male who looked like a fallen angel who worked out!

The fine lines around his marvellous eyes deepened as he looked down with concern into her face.

'Are you all right? There is someone you'd like me to call, perhaps?'

Oh, my God, even his voice was sexy! Deep and slightly gravelly, his cultured voice contained a faint and attractive foreign inflection.

'I…I…' She gulped, then he smiled and she thought, Wow!

Get a grip, girl. So you were smiled at by a good-looking man—there is no need to act as though you've just been released from a convent.

'You've had a shock. You're shaking…' Rafael pushed aside an intrusive flicker of genuine concern. Save it, he told himself, for Angelina and her marriage.

Besides, in his expert opinion this was about sex, not the sun or a blow to the head. He was not the only one to feel the sexual charge in the air. This was not a thing he could have anticipated, but Rafael knew that such things were easier to work with than fight against—not, obviously, to the extent that he followed the advice of the loud voice telling him that what he really wanted was *to know what she would taste like when he kissed her!*

Though had the circumstances been different, who knew…?

The comment drew Maggie's gaze to the fingers still curved around her upper arm. She made no attempt to break the contact; in fact she was conscious of a strange reluctance to do so.

She could feel the warmth in his long brown fingers through the thin fabric of her cotton top and sense the strength in them…in the man himself.

Her eyes lifted and the impression of strength she picked up from the light contact intensified. He was a big man, broad-shouldered and athletically built—he was both lean and hard.

He projected an undiluted force-field of raw masculinity. It was utterly overwhelming and…*seductive?*

The latter question made Maggie's eyes widen with shock. Curbing the imaginative dialogue in her head, she began to pull her arm away, then stopped as she encountered the flash of concern in his silver grey eyes.

She swallowed past the sudden emotional thickness in her throat and blinked as her eyelids prickled. She looked away, embarrassed by her emotional response to this cursory show of concern.

'I'm fine…oh!' Maggie grunted as a passerby bumped into her. 'Sorry…'

'*You* are sorry?' Her rescuer mumbled something under his breath and directed a glare of such autocratic outrage at the retreating back of the clumsy culprit that Maggie would not have been surprised to see the burly figure disintegrate into a pile of dust.

'You're very kind.'

Her low-pitched voice with the husky timbre came as a surprise—not an unpleasant one. 'You're English?'

Had he needed confirmation, this would have been it. He knew that Angelina had been shipped to England to have her baby.

She had not gone into details, but he could only imagine that the experience of being sent away from family and friends at such a time must have been a terrifying ordeal for a sixteen-year-old.

Maggie saw the flicker of expression move at the back of his incredible eyes and interpreted it as surprise. She had seen a lot of that when people realised she was not Spanish. There had been several occasions on this trip when unable to respond when, someone spoke to her in Spanish, she had had to explain that she was English.

It was difficult not to think about her genetic heritage when for the first time in her life her colouring made her blend in, not stand out.

She lifted a hand to smooth her tousled hair, a frown settling on her brow as she blinked to clear the unbidden image of Simon's excited expression when he had revealed that the firm he had employed to investigate her background *without telling her* had discovered her real mother did not have, as his own mother had suspected, Romany blood, but was in fact a member of one of Spain's oldest families.

'Like Mother said, it explains your temperament and your colouring, doesn't it, sweetheart? The way I see it,' he had mused, 'if this family are willing to acknowledge you it would do us no harm at all. Obviously we have to approach them sensitively…'

Sensitive—he actually said *sensitive* and with no trace of irony. 'You told your mother about this?'

Simon had remained oblivious to the danger in her voice and stilted manner. 'It was her idea.'

He had not appeared to notice her flinch as he'd smiled indulgently before announcing confidently, 'I know what you're thinking.'

Maggie had been pretty sure Simon hadn't or he wouldn't have been standing that close to her clenched fists.

She could remember clearly staring up at his handsome face, and thinking, I've never actually seen you before.

She was engaged to a man who didn't know her at all, a man who under the caring exterior he liked to cultivate, was utterly and totally self-centred.

'You're thinking how did the daughter of a Spanish aristocrat come to be adopted by an ordinary English couple.'

Maggie had recovered her voice in time to silence any further revelations and assure Simon that she had no interest in her birth mother or a family who were strangers to her, and neither did she have an interest in marrying him.

It had taken some time to convince Simon that she wasn't joking, but when he had realised he had been furious, revealing a side to his nature that she had never glimpsed previously.

Maggie flicked her ponytail firmly over her shoulder and equally firmly pushed away the memories.

She had moved on and in a rather unpredictable way, she thought, directing a bold direct stare at the face of the dark, devastatingly handsome Spaniard. Communication was not a problem; he spoke perfect English.

The problem was her inability to stop staring at him or speculate on how good his non-verbal communication skills were.

'You are here with your family?' He arched an ebony brow, his eyes travelling up from her toes to her glossy head.

She shook her head, feeling ridiculously tongue-tied and unable to shake the crazy conviction he could read her thoughts.

Rafael arched a dark slanted brow. 'Boyfriend…?'

Maggie rubbed the finger that had recently sported her engagement ring. 'No…'

Rafael's sharp gaze noted the action and he filed it away for future reference. She was young to be divorced, but he did not discount the possibility.

'I'm here alone. On holiday.' Nice move, Maggie—you've just told a total stranger that you're a vulnerable target. 'With friends,' she added quickly as her natural caution kicked in.

'You are alone with friends?'

She flushed and gave a self-conscious laugh and struggled not to look guilty. Her inability to lie without blushing remained a constant source of irritation. 'I'm with a group of friends,' she lied.

The corners of his sensual mouth lifted as he arched an ebony brow. 'Public place and I'm totally harmless,' he drawled, displaying an uncomfortable ability to read her mind as he stood there looking about as far removed from harmless as a wolf. She tilted her head back to look into his face and qualified further—of the big and bad variety.

'I'm sure you are,' she lied politely, adding, 'Excuse me,' as she fished her phone from her pocket and scanned last night's text from her mum with an expression of interest.

For some women, of course, the bad part would have been a plus, but she had never been drawn to danger. Danger was for women who could live in the moment, and men like him were for women who did not worry about how it would feel the next day.

Maggie had never been swept away by the moment, she had never said to hell with tomorrow and she didn't see the attraction of dangerous men any more than she felt the urge to walk along a crumbling cliff edge because the view was nice.

She studied her companion's dark lean face and couldn't deny that the view was very nice... The skin on her scalp tingled as her glance drifted to his mouth and she corrected her assessment. This man was many things but *nice* wasn't one of them!

Uncomfortably conscious of the flash of heat that washed over her skin, she pressed her hands to her stomach where a flock of butterflies were rioting and lowered her eyes back to her phone.

'Bad news?' he asked, not fooled by the little pantomime but playing dumb and for time.

His thoughts raced.

He needed to warn Angelina and give her the opportunity to tell Alfonso. He owed her that much, as he was the one who had encouraged her in her lie of omission to her husband in the first place.

That one had really come back to bite him, he reflected grimly. The next time he got asked for advice he would politely refuse.

This girl might, for all he knew, be an expert liar, but there were some things that you couldn't control and she was genuinely shaken. Whatever the cause it seemed logical to take advantage of it before she fully recovered her wits.

All he had to do was figure out in the next thirty seconds how to get her some place that wasn't here without breaking any laws... If it involved kissing that would be a plus, he reflected as his heated glance shifted to the full sexy curve.

'Not really...I just missed them.'

'Your many friends.'

Fascinated, he watched the colour rush over her cheeks.

She nodded, not meeting his eyes, but lifted her chin defiantly. 'We're meeting up back at the hotel,' she told him creatively before glancing at her watch and exclaiming, 'It's that time already!'

To her dismay the tall Spaniard did not take the hint; he just carried on looking at her. Looking hard. She lowered her own gaze. The unblinking regard was unsettling on more levels than she wanted to admit, let alone examine.

Maybe the novelty of a man noticing she existed had spooked her. Wincing at the self-pitying direction of her thoughts, she shook her head and laughed.

Rafael raised an enquiring brow. 'Something is funny?'

'Not funny—sad,' she admitted, hoping the enigmatic response would shut him up.

As he watched her soft lips curve into a determinedly cheerful smile that did nothing to banish the despondent shadow from her luminous eyes he felt feelings stir. Refusing to recognise them as concern—definitely not empathy—he reminded himself that his concern belonged with the mother and her threatened marriage, not the daughter.

He was attracted to the daughter—inconvenient, but not a problem. He had never had a problem keeping his libido on a leash. He couldn't allow himself to look at her and think of her as a beautiful woman because she was business and sex and business did not mix.

He had to look at her and think, Disaster waiting to happen.

While he could not *stop* the disaster unfolding, he could control the timing to minimise the impact and give Angelina time to tell her husband that she had a past and that that past had come calling.

There was a problem. Just one? mocked the voice in his skull. Every time he tried to focus on his strategy his train of thought got hijacked and he found himself thinking about her mouth.

He puzzled over this growing obsession.

It wasn't even as if she were as beautiful as Angelina. The resemblance was startling, but she was not, as he had first thought, a duplicate copy. Her face was heart-shaped and her nose, though delicate, was tip-tilted, her mouth was…

His thoughts slowed as his eyes drifted to that full, generous curve.

Her mouth, he admitted, was a problem.

He wanted to kiss her. The weakness angered him.

'Sad?'

Maggie shook her head. 'Just a private joke.' It was joke when she realised that she had allowed Simon to systematically undermine her confidence and make her feel that her wants and needs were always secondary to his.

It took a total stranger noticing her and being kind to bring home the extent to which she was hungry for attention and how invisible she had felt.

For Simon she had come just above…*maybe* above…his appointment with his hair stylist, because whether he liked it or not, as he was fond of telling her, the sad fact was that appearances counted in politics… The first time he had said this he had felt compelled to advise her that the amount of cleavage she was showing in her favourite red dress might give the wrong idea.

Her *blue* dress, he had added, made her look *wholesome.*

And she had been so eager to be the woman he wanted her to be that she had gone and changed, the same way she had stopped wearing her hair loose and had abandoned her killer heels.

Part of the problem was that she had been so young and impressionable when she met Simon, a first-year student on her first ward allocation, and the handsome son of a rather demanding patient had seemed very sophisticated.

And, yes, she had been flattered that he noticed her. For years boys had *not* noticed her, not really until the last year at school when she had finally said goodbye to the ubiquitous braces. The event had coincided with her skin clearing up, and, once revealed as smooth and flawless, her golden-toned complexion made her stand out among her fair-skinned classmates.

Her excess inches had also melted away almost overnight. She had needed a belt to keep her school skirt from falling down—she had a waist.

The boys at school had noticed her then, but their admiration had taken the form of crude comments and clumsy passes and Maggie, to hide her shyness, had responded to them with an icy disdain that had earned the not very inventive nickname of Ice Queen.

To Maggie at eighteen—and in her head still the dumpy teenager—Simon, a nearly-thirty-year-old lawyer with political ambitions, had seemed very sophisticated, and he had been interested in her!

He hadn't been clumsy, he'd been charming, and he had never made her feel awkward or uncomfortable. He had even been sympathetic when she confided how self-conscious her overgenerous breasts and curvy hips made her feel, patting her hand and assuring her comfortingly that nobody was *perfect*. With very limited experience of men and dating, Maggie had been relieved when he had put no pressure on her to go farther than kissing. Though the circumstances of her childhood had made her mature in many ways in other ways, she had led quite a sheltered life.

When he had asked her to marry him a dazzled Maggie had really believed herself in love and fully expected the relationship to move on to another level; her feelings about this had been mixed.

When Simon had said he respected her and he wanted to wait until they were married she was pretty sure that relief should not have figured even fleetingly in her reaction, but it had.

Her fists curled as she reflected angrily on how submissive she had been, how she had let Simon mould her into the person he wanted her to be.

'You wish to share this joke?'

Maggie shook her head. The last thing she wanted was to tell this man above all others that she was not used to male attention. She tried to frame a suitable excuse to make good her escape.

She could always just open her mouth and say, 'Go away,' but, having had good manners instilled in her from the cradle, it was hard for Maggie to tell anyone to get lost, especially when that someone had just sort of saved her life.

'Allow me to walk you back.'

Maggie shook her head and smiled to rob her refusal of offence. 'I couldn't possibly put you to the trouble.'

She thought of cliff edges and pretty views and sighed. No, she would definitely opt for the safe route even if the view was not so thrilling, although for a split second she had been tempted.

The same way you opted for the, oh, so safe Simon and that worked out so well.

Ignoring the contribution of the critic in her head, she folded her phone and held out her hand.

'Thank you very much for saving me, but I won't impose on you any longer.'

The stilted dismissal made Rafael veer between amusement and astonishment, then as his attention was captured by the rapid rise and fall of her rather magnificent breasts both were swallowed up by a blast of raw lust so strong he actually took a stiff half step backwards as his body hardened.

It took him unawares. It was a long time since he had wanted a woman this much, let alone a woman that was out of bounds... Maybe, he mused, that was the attraction...the forbidden fruit?

The fingers that tightened on her arm made her wince. He murmured an apology.

She couldn't see his expression; his heavy eyelids were lowered, leaving only a glittering slit of silver.

For a second she thought he wasn't going to take her hand, then he did, holding it a moment too long, giving time for the electrical tingle under her skin to morph into a shameful throb of awareness that clutched low like a fist in her belly.

Then his brown fingers tightened slightly before falling away.

She stayed motionless her eyes meshed with his compelling silver eyes. His gaze was strangely emotionless considering the electrical charge that shimmered in the air between them—or did it?

She brought her lashes down in an ebony protective screen and sucked in a shaky breath. She clearly needed to get her overactive imagination in line. It made no sense that the brush of a stranger's fingers could... She rubbed her hand against her thigh and dismissed the moment from her mind.

The sexual charge in the air did not diminish even though they were no longer touching.

'You are not well enough to walk.' It was not a lie; she looked pale and shaken.

'I'm fine. I just missed lunch and if I don't hurry I shall miss the paella evening.' Authentic, she reminded herself as she tried to work up enthusiasm for the prospect—the authentic flamenco evening had involved dancers who hailed from Manchester, though in their defence they had been very good.

'I know where they do the best paella.'

'How nice.'

He watched the appearance of the polite smile that was

starting to aggravate him and thought about doing something that would wipe it off her face.

'It would be nicer if I had company…would you come share some paella with me?'

CHAPTER FIVE

MAGGIE stared at Rafael, startled by the invitation.

'With you?' she asked, trying to judge if he was serious; not that it mattered—she was not going to say yes, was she?

His shoulders lifted in a magnificent shrug as he inclined his dark head.

Maggie gave a strained laugh and lifted her flushed face to his... So, all right, it was gratifying that a gorgeous man like this wanted her company, but not reality. 'I couldn't possibly...'

'Why not?'

'Because I don't know you...and I'm not...' she stumbled.

'Not?'

She gave him a direct look.

'You have very beautiful eyes.'

The eyes in question fell from his. 'You don't have to compliment me, and actually I don't like it.' Her heart was thudding so hard against her ribs that he had to hear it above the hum of the traffic.

'If that were true it would make you a very unusual woman, but as a matter of fact it was not a compliment.'

A laugh left Maggie's lips as her eyes swept upwards. 'No?' She arched a feathery brow. 'It definitely wasn't an insult.'

'You have a lot of experience of insults?'

Maggie smiled. 'I have brothers.'

He began to smile back, then as his eyes drifted to her mouth he stopped abruptly. The buzz of sexual awareness that had been pumping through his veins became a loud thrum.

'It was actually a statement of fact—you have very beautiful eyes.'

His eyes were resting on her mouth when he said it and something in the smoky scrutiny made Maggie's heart rate quicken.

And why not? She was allowed to be attracted to a man; it was plain silly to deny it. She was not expert at reading the signs, but it seemed possible he might be attracted to her, although he might be one of those men who were able to make every woman think she was special.

Attraction or not, it wasn't going anywhere. If she had been the sort of girl who could separate sex from emotion he would have been exactly the sort of man she would have chosen—she wondered uncomfortably if she had been sending out the wrong signals.

She gave an apologetic shrug and explained. 'I'm not looking for a holiday romance.'

Though some people had suggested—even her own mother had dropped hints—that this was exactly what she ought to be looking for.

Her friend Millie's typically outspoken parting shot came back to her.

'What you need to recover from Simon is some fun for once in your life—head-banging sex with no strings with, of course, the right stranger.'

Was there such a thing as the right stranger…and was he it? Maggie brought the train of thought, shocked, to an abrupt halt.

Her eyes widened. I am tempted. I'm really tempted!

He gave a sardonic smile. 'I was offering dinner.'

The mortified colour flew to her cheeks. 'Of course you were…sorry…that is, I was…' Wondering if no strings sex was such a terrible thing. And why shouldn't she? It wouldn't hurt anyone; it might even be liberating…it might even be fun.

She doubted this was the sort of fun her mum had had in mind.

He grinned, immediately achieving the impossible and looking even more rampantly gorgeous—he really was the most incredibly *male* man she had ever met—and looked amused.

'That is a yes.'

Flustered, Maggie swept the hair from her eyes. 'Yes, that is, no, I…'

'You wish for references perhaps?'

She flushed and shook her head feeling gauche, foolish and excited; her eyes widened in recognition of this last emotion. 'Of course not.'

'I am Rafael. Rafael-Luis Castenadas.' Holding her eyes, he bowed formally from the waist. He straightened, pushing a dark hank of hair back from his wide brow as he did so, then angled an enquiring brow and waited.

Not recognising the cue to give her own name, Maggie heard herself say, 'That's a lovely name.'

She squeezed her eyes closed and thought, Please, please, let the ground open up and swallow me.

He watched as she bit her lip hard enough to bruise the soft pink flesh and break the skin. He saw a bead of bright blood form and thought about blotting it with his tongue before… He stopped the thought but was unable to stop his body reacting lustfully to the image.

He had never met anyone with a more expressive face. Did

she allow every emotion she felt to register on those lovely features?

It made his task easier that she was so easy to read though he wondered how many men had taken advantage of her transparency—*as he was.*

He pushed aside the sliver of guilt. He had an excuse and he wasn't trying to get her into bed…though in other circumstances that might, he conceded, have been a tempting idea.

Maggie opened her eyes and found he was watching her; the unblinking intensity of his regard was unsettling.

'And you?' he prompted.

'Me?' she echoed, wondering about the expression she had glimpsed on his face.

'You have a name?'

She flushed and struggled to get her brain into gear. She could not believe the effect this total stranger was having on her. 'I'm Maggie. Maggie Ward, well, Magdalena really, but nobody calls me that.'

'Everyone starts out as strangers, Magdalena.'

His deep voice had a intimate quality. Maggie, uncomfortably conscious of the forbidden shiver trickling down her spine, told herself it was his accent. Just because he made her name sound exotic didn't mean she was—she was still the same Maggie who was far too sensible to get silly because a man with a pretty face and a more than all right body noticed she existed.

Her glance skimmed the long, lean, male length of him and the breath left her parted lips in a tiny sigh of appreciation that she hurriedly covered in a cough. Ruefully she admitted to herself he was better than all right—actually he was better than stupendous though a person would have to see him without the clothes to be sure.

Maggie stopped dead mid-speculation, her eyes widening to saucers. I'm mentally undressing a man!

'Even lovers…'

Her wide eyes leapt to his face. *'Lovers?'* she echoed, thinking if ever there was a cue to walk this was it. This was not a subject that total strangers discussed. His next comment made it clear he did not share her inhibitions. She was starting to think he might not have any.

'Lovers start out as strangers.'

He smiled at her with his eyes and her stomach flipped and quivered.

She recalled Millie's friendly advice on how to add some spice to her holiday.

'Act available, Maggie,' she had counselled. 'When your eyes meet his and your heart starts to thud and you get that delicious fluttery kick in your belly, don't look away. A guy needs some encouragement.'

Maggie took a deep breath and didn't look away.

It was just dinner, there would be other people, and she'd be experiencing some of the local culture, which was what she liked about foreign travel.

'Will they have room at this paella place?'

Just for once it would be good to break away from her sensible image—not too far, obviously. And they were not talking the head banging, no-strings sex thing—this was dinner.

Where would be the harm?

As his strangely hypnotic eyes swept slowly across her upturned features. It probably made her pathetic, but she really wished she'd put on more make-up than a swipe of lip gloss and a smudge of eyeshadow.

As he examined the fine-boned features Rafael was struck once more by the startling resemblance between mother and daughter, but now he was equally conscious of the dissimilarities. The younger woman would be considered by most to have less claim to classical beauty, but when it came to sex appeal she was streets ahead.

'They will always make room for me. Come…'

No shocker that he should issue commands—he had that written all over him. The shock was that she allowed him to steer her through the throng.

Looking back on the moment and the ones that followed later, Maggie was left to wonder if her body had not been taken over by an alien.

Maggie paused, ducking her head to look through the door he held open for her. The sumptuous interior looked just as impressive as the exterior of the long, low, powerful-looking car.

'This is yours?'

'You are going to lecture me on my carbon footprint or car theft?'

She slung him a cross glance and slid inside, lifting the newspaper that lay on the passenger seat. The headline was in Spanish but the image was one that had graced several front pages across the world that week—a well-known Hollywood star with his long-term partner making their relationship official at a civil ceremony.

The image of the two hand-in-hand, smiling men shifted her thoughts back to her dad's parting words when Maggie had been startled to realise that her dad, at least, had his own ideas about what had caused her to break off the engagement.

'I respect the fact you don't want to talk about it, love, but the fact is, Maggie, some men…just because Simon has issues with his…*leanings*…'

Maggie had stared, astonished, as her father, red-faced, had cleared his throat before finishing huskily. 'Never think you were the problem or it was your fault.'

'No,' she had responded faintly, thinking, Was I the only one who didn't have a clue?

And she hadn't—not until that final argument when things had got pretty ugly.

Maggie had never seen the normally restrained Simon so angry before, and the trigger to him losing it totally had of all things been a throwaway comment in the heat of the moment, because he didn't have the faintest idea *why* she was angry. 'I don't think you even *like* women!'

'Who have you been listening to? I am *not* gay!'

Before Maggie had been able to assure him she hadn't meant that at all he had grabbed her arm and wrenched her towards him, lowered his face to her and snarled, 'If you spread lies like that I'll…'

Startled by his aggressive reaction, Maggie had frozen with shock, but had not lowered her gaze from his menacing glare. She knew from past experience it was a mistake to show fear to bullies. And Simon was a bully.

Why had she not known that before?

Anger had come to her rescue; her chin had come up and she had asked with cold disdain, 'You'll what, Simon?'

The ruddy colour rising up his neck had reached his cheeks, darkening the skin to magenta as he'd glared at her in furious frustration. 'I…I'll…'

Pretending not to notice the fingers tightening painfully around her wrist, she had cut across him. 'Look, I'm sorry if I touched a raw nerve, but your sexuality is not a subject that interests me.'

Simon had looked at the ring she held out to him and released her arm.

She had dropped it into his palm, walked away and not looked back.

Maggie threw the newspaper into the back seat and fastened her belt with a click. Her chin lifted. Being sensible had got her nothing but humiliation; it was time for a bit of recklessness.

But maybe not this much, she thought half an hour later as they seemed to finally arrive at their destination. The village cut into the hillside was small, in a matter of moments they had driven through.

Keeping her voice carefully casual, Maggie turned her head in time to see the village lights disappear as the road began to climb steeply and asked, 'Aren't we stopping?'

Maggie recognised the extreme vulnerability of her position; she was in a car miles from anywhere with a man who could, for all she knew, be a homicidal maniac and nobody knew where she was.

She should be seriously scared, so why wasn't she?

'Relax, Maggie, I'm quite harmless.'

She looked at his profile and thought, If you were I wouldn't be here. It was a bit late to recognise that it was the danger he represented that had drawn her here.

He was her rebellion against the self-imposed rules she had lived her life by.

'Relax—you will enjoy yourself, you know.' She looked at him with big wary eyes and he expelled a sigh. 'That was not a threat, you know, and you can take your hand off the door—it's locked.'

'Why didn't we stop in the village?'

'Because,' he said, pulling the car onto a patch of rocky ground beside a number of other vehicles, 'the villagers are all here.' He released the central lock. 'You are sorry now that you came?'

Maggie, her lips curved in a happy smile, shook her head. 'No.' When he'd said the village was here he had not been exaggerating; the area of flat ground fringed by trees was full of people.

She felt his eyes on her and turned her head.

Her own smile faded as their glances connected and locked.

The raw hunger in his deep-set eyes made her breath quicken and her stomach muscles quiver receptively.

For a moment their glances clung until Maggie, her heart beating hard, allowed her lashes to fall in a concealing veil.

The heavy thrum of her pounding blood in her ears was deafening. Confused, excited and scared by the strength of her reaction she ran ahead, anxious to distance herself from him and her feelings.

She used the moment to gather her calm around her like a comfort blanket—she wasn't *comforted* but after a little deep breathing she was able to speak without babbling anything stupid like, 'You're beautiful,' when he reached her side.

The tremors that hit her body intermittently she could do little about, so she jammed her hands in the pockets of her jeans, blissfully unaware that while the first-aid measure hid her shaking hands it also pulled the denim tight across her bottom, riveting Rafael's eyes on the feminine flare of her hips.

'This is incredible,' she said, not feigning her enthusiasm as she looked around the mountainside clearing. 'However did you find this place?'

Eyes shining, Maggie stared at the scene, drinking it in: the flickering flames of the open fires, smoke in the night, the strings of fairy lights in the tall pines twinkling above the heads of the people of all ages sitting at the rustic tables, eating, drinking, laughing and some dancing to the music supplied by an accordion player.

The smell of the food cooking in the giant pots filled the air and mingled with the wood smoke, the scent of damp grass, and the wild thyme crushed underfoot.

'Rafael.' The man who greeted her companion stared at Maggie with open curiosity before smiling and making a comment in his native tongue.

The men spoke for a moment before Rafael turned back to

Maggie. 'I did not find it,' he said, responding to her previous question. 'I was brought up not far from here.'

'A country boy!'

He arched a dark brow as he placed his fingers under her elbow to guide her to a seat at one of the long trestle tables. 'That surprises you?'

Considering his aura of sophistication it did, but she had to admit he did seem very relaxed and at home in the surroundings and, judging by the number of people who greeted him with warmth and familiarity, he had not forgotten his roots.

She smiled as people moved to make way for them; Rafael told her to save him a seat while he left to bring her back food.

Maggie sat quietly drinking in the sights and smells, trying to commit this very special moment to memory, she was pretty sure that by the morning it would all seem like a dream.

Rafael returned carrying two plates of steaming paella and, setting one before her, pulled a stray chair to the table and straddled it.

Maggie speared a prawn with her fork and put it in her mouth. She gasped. 'That is incredible!' and refilled her fork.

Her plate was half empty when she realised that Rafael was spending more time watching her than eating himself.

She lifted her eyes to his face and once again he responded to a question before she had framed it. 'I like watching you eat. It is rare to see a woman who enjoys her food.'

'Well, I'd enjoy it more if you weren't watching every mouthful,' she admitted frankly.

Maggie tapped her foot as the fiddler struck up a fresh tune. The man on the accordion finished off his glass of wine before he joined in too. There was a ripple of clapping as people flocked onto the makeshift dance floor. This was clearly a popular choice.

'They all look as if they're having a good time.'

The wistful note in her voice was not lost on Rafael, who was starting to find her undisguised enthusiasm for everything wearing. Every time she looked at him with wide trusting eyes he experienced a need to justify his actions to himself that he did not enjoy.

He knew he was doing the right thing.

So why, asked the voice in his head, do you feel like such a lowlife?

'The paella is very lovely.'

Of course it was.

She was the easiest woman to please he had ever met and by far the most beautiful.

Would she be equally appreciative in bed?

The sybaritic image of her naked body beneath him, her dark hair spread out on a pillow, flashed into his head. Struggling to banish the erotic sequence of images that followed it, he shut his eyes, disconcerted by the strength of the desire that gripped him.

It seemed the moment to remind himself that she was not his type at all.

Luscious, obviously, but there was an aura of wide-eyed innocence about her that under normal circumstances he would have steered well clear of.

He had a low boredom threshold and virtue was, in his experience, boring. It was admittedly not boredom that had him in a constant state of painful arousal, but sexual hunger once quenched did not have a long shelf life. He gave a jaundiced smile; if anyone knew that it was him.

Maybe, he mused, it was genetic. His father's numerous mistresses had never lasted long—pride in his family name had not extended to Felipe Castenadas depriving himself of female companionship after Rafael's mother's departure.

There had been many women and his father had spoken about them with a lack of respect behind their backs and sometimes to their faces that had never sat easily with Rafael as a boy.

Rafael had been in his early teens when he had gone to leave the room in disgust during the middle of one of his father's coarse diatribes about his mistress of the moment.

His father had stood up and blocked the door. Rafael could still recall the smell of alcohol on his breath. 'You know what your problem is, boy, you romanticise women,' he had sneered. 'Don't shake your head, boy, I'm doing you a favour. Do you want a woman to make a fool of you? At heart they are all like your mother, basically whor—'

The crude sentence had never been completed. Felipe had met his son's eyes—realising for the first time perhaps that he had to tilt his head to do so—and what he had seen there had made him pale.

He had moved away from the door maintaining an illusion of macho bluster, but clearly shaken. It had been a turning point. He had never pushed Rafael in the same way, or mentioned his mother again.

In other respects nothing had changed. It wasn't just female companionship his father had not deprived himself of—Felipe Castenadas had lived a lavish lifestyle even when he couldn't afford it. Rafael had been forced to watch silently as his father sold off the estate he'd claimed to love piece by piece to pay for his indulgences, all the time silently vowing to one day restore it.

He had done so now and gained in the process the respect and gratitude of the people on the estate. Though his father would never have accepted an invite to a party like this, Rafael did so regularly, and he frequently enjoyed these simple occasions more than the lavish social events he was expected to attend.

He had never brought anyone along before so he could almost see the speculation in his tenants' faces as they looked at his companion. It was annoying but the speculation would die away.

He studied her through his lashes as she smiled. The man who did end up with her would have to share her—the woman loved the whole world, and paella.

He watched as her smile had a predictable effect on a group of young men who stood a few feet away, staring. He could almost smell the testosterone from here; she remained cheerfully oblivious to the effect it had on them.

Rafael's clenched teeth were starting to ache.

If that smile had turned out to conceal a mean and spiteful agenda he might not be feeling this uncharacteristic guilt.

He had nothing to feel guilty about.

So why do you feel the need to remind yourself of that so frequently?

'You are not counting carbs, then?'

The sardonic observation made Maggie lift her chin. 'Sorry if that offends you,' she said, sounding anything but.

'It was not a criticism.'

Almost certain that, despite this reassurance, it was exactly that, Maggie paused, her fork in the air. The furrow between her brows deepened as she studied his dark face. His entire attitude since they had arrived had been offhand and she was getting the impression he had regretted bringing her.

She ought to be regretting it too, but the hormonal rush she got every time she looked at him had an addictive quality. Then there was the smell of his skin and the way he... She inhaled deep, closing down this chain of thought, which could, if left unchecked, go on for a long time—there was a lot about him she found fascinating!

He might be her hormonal Achilles' heel, but she was not about to apologise for liking food. She had been there, done that before.

'I tried dieting.' Simon had bought her a number of very

useful books on the subject of healthy eating. 'It made me cranky and I almost fainted running for the bus.'

A look of astonishment crossed his face. 'Why would you diet?' His eyes dropped, sliding appreciatively over her lush curves; by the time he made the return journey to her face Maggie's cheeks were burning and her heart was slamming hard against her ribs like a trapped bird.

She was trapped, trapped by the sheer strength of the sexual awareness that had invaded every cell of her body.

'I know I could do with losing my hips and my bottom is a bit…'

A hoarse rattling sound emerged from Rafael's throat. 'You have a magnificent body.'

Heat flashed through her body as their eyes meshed, the sweet sharp ache between her legs made Maggie shift uncomfortably and feel acutely embarrassed—but mingled with the embarrassment was a strong element of dizzy excitement.

'Clothes hide a multitude of sins,' she joked, trying to lower the sexual temperature, she was mortified by the thought of anyone listening in to this conversation.

'It depends on your definition of sin.' His slurred drawl made her shiver. 'Would you like to compare notes?'

Maggie swallowed, the fork slipping from her nerveless fingers. His smoky eyes were eating her up.

'I would really like to know what sinful thoughts are going through that beautiful head right now.' His finger trailed down her cheek.

Maggie gasped and pulled back breaking the spell that held her in sexual thrall. 'I'd really like to dance.'

Rafael laughed at the change of subject and thought I would like to see what those clothes are hiding. 'This is not my sort of music.'

'Your foot was tapping.' Perhaps it was just her he didn't want to dance with?

He heaved a sigh, there was time to ring Angelina and warn her later.

And why should he pass up the opportunity to legitimately hold that soft warm body next to his own?

It looked as if he was not the only person to have this idea.

Recognising the young man who, egged on by shouts from his friends lining the makeshift bar, was approaching, Rafael acknowledged him. 'Enrique.'

The friends, who clearly had not really thought their friend this bold, fell silent.

Maggie watched as the two men spoke; the young man with the bold eyes and macho swagger kept flashing her smouldering looks that made her want to laugh. Despite the physical dissimilarities—he was dark and not very tall; Sam and Ben were tall and fair—he reminded her of her brothers.

When Rafael showed any inclination to smoulder in her direction she felt no desire to smile—in fact her reaction was worryingly close to throwing herself on the floor and screaming, *Take me!*

There had to be a logical reason for her bizarre behaviour... That fish last night had tasted funny...?

'Enrique wants to know if you'd like to dance.'

'And you don't mind?'

His brows lifted at the question. 'Why should I mind?' Rafael shrugged, displaying zero reluctance to relinquish her to the care of the flashing-eyed young man, and said, 'Have fun.'

Maggie looked at him with narrowed eyes. Weren't Spanish men meant to be possessive? Clearly if they were Rafael was the exception to the rule because, far from objecting to the handsome boy—actually he was more than a boy; now she looked more closely she could see he was probably nearer her own age than her brothers', but next to Rafael there was something immature about him—

'Don't worry, I will,' she promised, taking the young man's hand and allowing him to lead her out onto the dance floor.

CHAPTER SIX

RAFAEL drummed HIS fingers impatiently on the table-top as he waited for Angelina to pick up. He felt a jolt as Maggie, who appeared to be rapidly losing her inhibitions, turned her head and smiled at him.

He smiled back, then scowled as she was whirled away by her laughing partner, her dark hair streaming behind her like a silken cloud, her laughter floating on the air as Enrique, his shirt unfastened to reveal a bronzed chest, pulled her closer to demonstrate a complicated step that she copied with ease.

She was very graceful and her laughter and her lack of inhibition made him feel unaccountably annoyed.

Above the sound of her warm laughter he heard Angelina's voice.

'Rafael, are you at a party? Is that why you deserted us so early? Alfonso said you were avoiding the photos.'

Rafael forced his gaze from the dancing couples.

'I'm planning on staying at the *castillo* tonight. Is Alfonso there?'

'Yes, do you want to speak to him?'

'No. Don't talk, just listen.' I'm about to turn your perfect day into a nightmare. He expelled a deep breath and said, 'Your daughter is here.'

The silence lasted a full thirty seconds before she breathed hoarsely, 'That isn't possible! What is she like, Rafael?'

'Like you,' he said, wishing he could not hear the raw longing in her voice. Conscious of a male voice in the background, sharp with concern he added quickly, 'She was going to crash the party.' The ease with which he had diverted her had made Rafael think that the timing of her arrival might after all have been fortuitous—from her point of view—rather than malicious.

Malicious or not, the effect would have been equally destructive. He did not regret his actions and the necessary subterfuge. This was definitely a moment when the ends justified the means.

'I'm playing it by ear,' he admitted. 'I don't think she knows who I am.'

A man who believed in meticulous research, Rafael did not enjoy the novel sensation of working in the dark.

If he'd had a detailed report on his laptop telling him everything that was relevant about Miss Maggie Ward, he would have been much happier. At the moment all he knew about her was that she had a lopsided smile, a husky voice, a mouth that invited sinful speculation and a lush distracting body—and she liked paella.

'If the opportunity arises and she feels able to confide in me I will do my best to convince her this is a bad move, but that's a long shot,' he admitted, thinking of the stubborn firmness of her rounded chin. 'You should tell Alfonso sooner rather than later. I'm sorry, Angelica, it was bad advice.'

He slid the phone into his pocket as a breathless and happy Maggie was delivered by a smug-looking Enrique back to the table.

Maggie, her face flushed from the exertion and her eyes sparkling, smiled as the young man spoke, then looked to Rafael.

'What did he say?' Without waiting for the translation she caught Enrique's hand and flashed a smile of radiant warmth, then, appearing oblivious to the effect it had on the susceptible boy, said, 'That was fantastic. You're a great dancer, but I'm worn out,' she added, fanning herself with her hand and miming a faint.

The young man raised her hand to his lips and spoke again.

'He said that you not only look beautiful but you dance beautifully too.'

'Oh, how sweet!' Maggie said raising herself on her tiptoes to reach up to plant a kiss on the young man's smooth cheek. She turned her head to Rafael, her smile fading as she encountered his stony expression. 'Tell him thank you.'

'He already got that part.' A nerve clenched in his lean cheek as Rafael sought to contain the irrational surge of anger that he had experienced when he had watched her kiss the boy.

'I think he's smitten.'

Maggie's eyes narrowed and her chin lifted at the cold criticism in his manner. She refused point-blank to allow him to make her feel guilty for a spontaneous peck on the cheek, it had just been innocent fun and even if it hadn't been it was none of his business!

It wasn't as if he had wanted to dance with her. Now that, she admitted, would have been a very different experience and not nearly so innocent.

'That's because I'm utterly irresistible, a real man-eater.'

Rafael said something that drew a laugh from the young man who caught Maggie's hand, bowed low over it and brushed it with his lips. Then with a grin and a display of youthful exuberance he ran off to be clapped on the shoulder by his friends before claiming his next partner.

Antipathy shone in Maggie's eyes as she took her seat next to Rafael. Choosing water rather than wine, she filled her glass from one of the jugs on the table.

He raised a brow at her choice and taunted lightly, 'The vintage not to your palate?' The locally made wine, thanks to some clever marketing, had actually started to appear on a number of high-end restaurant wine lists, and his investment in the new winery that many had considered wasteful had not only already paid for itself but brought jobs to an area where young people were often forced to leave in order to find work.

'You're not drinking,' Maggie observed, unwilling to admit she had no head for alcohol—a sniff of a wine gum made her tipsy.

'I'm driving.'

The reminder made her frown. 'What time is it?'

He extended his arm towards her; his sleeve was rolled up to the elbow. Maggie stared for a moment, her throat dry and her heart pounding as she struggled to resist the impulse to run her fingers over the hair that lightly dusted his sinewed golden forearm.

Her voice was husky as she read the time on the metal-banded watch that circled his wrist out loud.

'It's a long way back,' she fretted.

Rafael watched as she nibbled gently at the pouting curve of her full lower lip. This had never been about seduction…but he found himself wanting her more than he had wanted a woman in a very long time.

'Don't look so worried—I am a man who believes that a woman is allowed to change her mind.' This was an attitude that had rarely been tested.

The colour flew to Maggie's cheeks. 'About what?'

He just laughed. 'It's fine if you have second thoughts,' he observed not in reality feeling at all fine as he looked at her lovely mouth. His glance slid lower to the outline of her lush breasts beneath the fine fabric of her top, and he felt even less fine.

He felt hungry.

She didn't know whether to be relieved by his take-it-or-leave-it attitude or insulted.

Had she changed her mind?

Did she have a mind? Now the initial defiant mood had ebbed, allowing herself to be picked up by a total stranger had started to seem less spontaneous and more criminally reckless.

And if she felt this way when the music was playing and the moon was shining how was she going to feel in the morning? she asked herself.

There had to be a less dramatic way to shake her sensible girl image. Next time she would settle for something tamer, like a motorbike or tattoos.

'I will make sure you get safely back.' Maggie's eyes connected with his and her stomach went into a lurching dive. There was nothing safe about the glow in his smoky eyes. 'But what,' he asked, tilting his chair back to avoid a collision with some passing dancers, 'is the hurry?'

Enrique called out and winked at her as he whirled his new partner past.

'What did you say to him before?' she asked suspiciously. 'Were you talking about me?'

'I simply translated.'

Maggie replayed the conversation and her eyes widened in dismay. 'You didn't!'

One corner of his mouth lifted in a mocking smile. 'Actually I gave him a modified version—I told him that you eat little boys like him for breakfast.'

'What if he thought you were serious?' she charged.

His eyes dropped and Maggie was shocked and embarrassed to feel her body respond to the slow, insolent sweep of his densely lashed eyes.

'What makes you think I was not serious?' he countered. His voice lowered a husky octave as he leaned into her and observed softly, 'You are a very desirable woman.'

Tongue-tied and blushing, she looked away, unable to come up with a smart remark to diffuse the fizz of sexual tension.

Did she want to diffuse it?

A thoughtful expression drifted across his lean predatory features as Rafael watched her plunge into a state of delicious blushing confusion. Rather than exploiting her sexuality, she seemed shocked by any reference to it.

'I think maybe I will have some more to eat.' Not looking at him, Maggie picked up her plate.

As she hurried across the grass towards the long trestle table loaded with food she bit her lip to repress a groan. So much for the new improved sexy me—I must have looked like a scared rabbit! What must he think of me?

Unable to stop herself, she glanced back over her shoulder and it became clear he wasn't thinking of her at all. Her place had been taken by a pretty woman in a low-cut blouse who as Maggie watched threw back her head and laughed, her uninhibited spontaneity a striking contrast to Maggie's own stilted self-consciousness.

She felt a stab of something that was obviously not jealousy but was nonetheless unpleasant. It was strange. She was not normally so self-conscious; it was just something about Rafael... Something? Who was she kidding? It was everything about Rafael!

The fact was she had never been attracted to a man this way in her life before. It wasn't just the fact he was incredibly handsome, which he was, it was more...his earthy sensuality... She shook her head, frustrated by her inability to analyse what it was about him.

Maybe it was not possible to analyse; maybe she just had to accept that looking at his mouth made her ache.

One minute she was thinking about his carnal perfect mouth and the things she was shocked to realise she would have liked him to do to her with it and the next she was running.

Later, when she tried to work out the exact sequence of events they remained a confused jumble. In each reconstruction her shocking, shameful thoughts somehow mixed up with the sense of panic and urgency that she reacted to instinctively.

She was never even sure why she had glanced towards a pile of recently sawn timber—perhaps movement caught her eye? She actually looked away, barely registering it as her attention drifted to the children playing a hundred yards or so away.

Then a low rumble just audible above the sounds of merriment made her turn her head again. She froze, paralysed with horror as she saw the stack of felled trees begin to move... Like a house of cards they slipped, fell and began to roll down the steep incline.

Straight towards the group of playing children.

The plate slipped from her fingers. She was told later she yelled—that was what caught the attention of the others who set off in her wake—but she had no memory of that. She just remembered running, praying and the sound of her laboured breathing loud in her ears as she raced towards the children.

By the time she reached them the older ones, alerted by cries, had already started moving, running out of the path of the approaching danger. Some were crying, but the sound was lost in the general pandemonium.

Maggie bent and scooped up two of the smaller children sprinting to the safety of higher ground before depositing them in the arms of women standing, shocked, watching, and she went back, passing men running in the opposite direction with children in their arms.

One child remained, a solemn-eyed little boy who raised his arms to Maggie when she reached him, hefting him into her arms. She turned, pressed his face into her shoulder and tried to run; her legs felt leaden. They worked painfully slowly as she fought against the inertia, struggling to suck air into her oxygen-starved lungs.

She could hear the danger approaching but didn't dare look... Convinced she wasn't going to make it with her last ounce of strength she flung the little boy at a young man who was running out to meet them.

She saw him safe and closed her eyes as the adrenaline rush in her bloodstream dipped dramatically. She tried to run felt her legs give and cried out. Safety was tantalisingly near but she couldn't... Her face scrunched into a teeth-clenched mask of determination as she tried to push herself forward.

Then something hit her. For a brief moment she thought it was the loose timber, then she realised the solidity was warm and male—it was Rafael. She stopped fighting as he carried her from danger.

CHAPTER SEVEN

THE impetus of Rafael's sprint carried them both past the crowd of cheering villagers and to the brink of the grassy slope beyond. He dug his heels in but the momentum he had built up was too great to resist and they went over the top, Maggie still in his arms.

As they landed at the bottom the breath left her body in a painful whoosh as she sank into the mercifully soft ground. For a moment she couldn't breathe or speak…but euphoria made her want to explode. She was alive—that was a big, a massive, plus considering the way things had been looking seconds earlier. A little detail like speech loss was fine, bruises were fine, Rafael on top of her was…

Her chaotic thoughts slowed from a breathless gallop to a slow canter. Rafael was on top of her!

He was breathing like a marathon runner. She was underneath him, a position that if she was honest she had been imagining pretty much from the second she saw him.

She felt fingers frame her chin and heard a deep voice harsh with concern ask, 'Are you all right, Maggie? Can you hear me?'

'Of course I can hear you. I'm not deaf.' She opened her eyes, his face suspended above her was very close.

His heavy-lidded eyes blazed, the heat in them pinning her

as surely as his body; the bones of his face stood out in stark prominence beneath his gleaming golden skin.

She got breathless and it had nothing to do with his weight pinning her down—well, only partly. The veneer of cultured civilisation and urbane charm was totally stripped away, revealing the essence of the raw masculinity beneath.

Without a word or taking his eyes from her, he bent his head and fitted his mouth to hers, kissing her hard, then without a word he rolled off her.

'You went back?'

She turned her head in response to the stark incredulity in his voice. Rafael lay on his back, one arm curved above his head, staring at the sky. She could see his chest rising and falling in sync with his laboured inhalations.

She decided that if he could pretend the kiss hadn't happened, so could she. She could definitely ignore the fact her lips tingled and his taste was in her mouth, a piece of cake!

'I think you saved my life, thank you.' Twice, if anyone was counting.

She expected him to mention the fact.

He didn't.

'I don't want your thanks.'

She lay there on the floor as he got to his feet in one lithe athletic bound. He dragged the hair back from his brow before extending a hand.

After a pause Maggie took it and found herself hauled to her feet.

'You insane idiot, do you have a death wish?'

Maggie was spared from responding to this savage question because at that moment the village en masse swept over them like a blanket of goodwill and concern.

Maggie was carried away on a wave of hugs, kisses and tears, taken quite literally to the heart of the village.

She was declared a heroine bilingually. It was all very

emotional and Maggie, both embarrassed and overwhelmed by the attention, went very quiet.

She lost count of the number of times she said she was fine. It was Rafael who finally rescued her from the love and adulation, saying firmly that she needed rest, could they not all see that she was about to collapse?

She repressed her natural inclination to deny she was that pathetic and allowed herself to be escorted back to his car. It seemed to Maggie from his manner that Rafael's intervention was motivated more by irritation than concern for her well-being.

He had received his share of gratitude too and with every thank-you his mood seemed to have got darker.

Was she paranoid or was she the focus of his annoyance?

Maybe he was actually hurt but was too macho to admit it. She had got the definite impression when they were falling that he was trying to shield her using his body and his arms, which had circled her like a steel barrier to cushion the impact.

And despite his assurances to the contrary the cuts on his dark face did suggest he hadn't escaped as lightly as she had. His dark hair was tousled and his shirt was ripped almost off his back, revealing a very distracting expanse of brown chest, well-developed shoulders and flat, muscle-ridged belly, not to mention a hand-sewn label that explained in part his irritation: his shirt was no more off the peg than his body was.

Maybe he blamed her for everything, including the ripped shirt. She thought about the angry kiss—hard not to—her eyes half closing as she remembered the texture of his firm lips, the warmth of his breath…the brief explosion of mind-numbing passion.

It was lucky, really, that everyone had assumed her numbed state was caused by the trauma of the accident. She wanted them to carry on believing this version. For Rafael to even suspect that a kiss that had barely registered on his radar had turned her the next best thing to catatonic would have been too mortifying.

She lifted a hand to her mouth and tilted her head back to catch a glimpse of his beautiful sculpted mouth, and immediately stumbled on the rocky ground where the cars, including Rafael's, had been parked.

Several pairs of arms reached to catch her but Rafael's were there first. Ignoring her weak protest, he swung her up into his arms, barely breaking stride.

Reaching his car, he deposited her in the front seat.

'That was quite unnecessary,' she said frostily.

'You are welcome.' He inclined his dark head, his grey eyes mocking her.

Maggie managed a stiff smile as one of the women placed a blanket over her knees. The man standing beside the woman waited until she had tugged it snugly around Maggie before he leaned into the car and clasped one of Maggie's hands between both of his and said something in Spanish.

Maggie gave a helpless smile and the old man looked to Rafael.

'The little boy you went back for was Alfredo's grandson. He says to tell you that you are an angel sent from God.'

Maggie gave an embarrassed little shrug, then turning her hand to grasp the teak-coloured gnarled fingers that lay on top of hers, she squeezed and smiled saying huskily, 'I'm glad nobody was hurt.' She glanced at Rafael, bit her lip and, struggling to control the husky throb of emotion in her voice, said, 'Tell him what I said, please.'

Rafael's eyes lingered on her face, moving up in a sweep from the graceful line of her slender neck, the curve of her cheek, the fullness of her lips and her wide-spaced liquid dark eyes. Alfredo's description seemed apt—she did look like an angel, a sad, sexy angel.

This was a situation where seeing both sides of the

argument was not useful. Maggie Ward might have many excellent qualities beyond a kissable mouth and a sinfully sexy body, but he didn't want to know about them. It confused the issue.

She was a danger to the happiness of two people he cared about. Focus on that, he told himself, and forget about her mouth and her courage. Think of her as a problem to be solved and maybe a pleasurable interlude.

And why not? Why was he beating himself up because he found her attractive? He knew the attraction was reciprocated. He was in danger of letting her innocent aura make him lose sight of the facts. He had not kidnapped her, drugged her or sworn eternal love; she had come of her own free will.

Maggie Ward knew that his intentions were strictly dishonourable and she had come along anyway. She was a young woman who wanted to add the spice of a one-night stand to her trip, so why should he feel as though he was taking advantage?

He had been staring at her so long that it crossed Maggie's mind that for some inexplicable reason he might be about to refuse her request.

'Please?'

Responding to the prompt and ignoring the questioning look in her eyes, Rafael translated.

Maggie watched the elderly man's lined face crease into a wide smile as he listened to Rafael. He turned his attention back to Maggie, said fervently, *'Angel.'* And pressed something into her hand before bowing out of the car to join the other villagers who had gathered to say goodbye.

'Watch the door.'

Maggie responded to the abrupt instruction and pulled the blanket closer as Rafael slammed the passenger door with what seemed to her like unnecessary force. There was nothing in his manner to suggest he agreed with the other man's version of her actions. Now she was sure it wasn't her imagination—his attitude towards her since the accident had been terse and unfriendly to a degree that could not be due to a spoiled designer shirt.

Any inclination to flirt with her had presumably vanished along with her make-up and hairgrips. He was obviously a man who could not see past dirty faces.

Or maybe his taste didn't run to angels?

She had no idea why she felt so let down. It wasn't as if she had been thinking of him as deep and meaningful when she looked at him, though a bit of dust on his face had not lessened his magnetism, she admitted, sliding a covert peek at his dark face.

But then it was hard to think of anything that would.

Slightly embarrassed, she waved back to the crowd that had gathered as the car drew away. As they vanished from view she opened her hand.

'Oh,' she gasped. 'I can't take this.' The gold medallion resting in her palm was obviously old; the carving was delicate. 'It must be valuable.' She held it out towards Rafael.

'It's a Saint Christopher.'

'I know. Take me back. I must return it.'

Rafael did not respond to her urgent request. 'You can't do that—it would offend him.'

'But…'

'He wanted you to have it.'

'I'm a stranger,' she protested.

'A stranger who saved his grandson's life, his *angel*.' And was she anybody else's angel? he wondered. Was there a man back home who would not be pleased that she had driven off into the mountains with a stranger?

She wore no ring, but that didn't mean she was unattached. For some women a man back home did not prevent them indulging in a holiday romance, though for some reason he was struggling to put her in that bracket.

The mockery in his voice brought Maggie's chin up. Her fingers tightened around the medallion. His cynical sarcasm made her see red. 'You shouldn't make fun of him,' she said fiercely.

'I wasn't making fun of *him*. I couldn't help but notice you were enjoying the attention.'

This totally unfair scathing evaluation took Maggie's breath away. 'And their heirlooms, don't forget that. I managed to fleece them too.' She allowed her dark eyes to move contemptuously over his patrician profile before putting the medallion over her head. She freed her tangled hair from the chain. 'You do know that you are a very unpleasant man, don't you?'

'Is that why you let me pick you up?'

Colour scored her pale cheeks. 'I made a mistake and assumed you couldn't be as shallow and superficial as you appeared—I was wrong. And you sulk.'

The bitter afterthought drew a startled look from Rafael.

'I'd be happier having cheated death once today if you kept your eyes on the road.'

'*Sulk?*' Accustomed to hearing the women in his life express rapturous praise, Rafael struggled to swallow this more critical analysis of his character.

On any other occasion his utter astonishment at the accusation might have drawn a smile from Maggie.

'Well, you're obviously in a strop over something, but I'd be grateful if you didn't take it out on me.'

They had passed through the village before reaction hit her. She started to shake. She tugged the blanket closer and made a clinical diagnosis of delayed shock.

'Are you cold?' Rafael asked, adjusting the heating.

Biting back a childish, 'Like you'd care' she compressed her lips and said coldly, 'I'm fine.'

'Then why are you shaking?'

She was bewildered by his continued hostility and accusing manner. Did he think she was acting?

Determined to give him no opportunity to accuse her of being an attention seeker or canvassing the sympathy vote she plastered on a cheery smile.

'I'm not,' she denied. 'I feel fine.' It was only a very small lie, actually. Other than her shaking hands and the scratches on her arm that were stinging she really didn't feel too bad, and she would feel a lot better once this man was a distant memory.

She was a very bad liar, though even a good liar, Rafael thought, his eyes flickering briefly in her direction, would have struggled to deny the chattering teeth and milky pallor.

Accustomed to the company of women who did not know the meaning of 'putting on a brave face,' he realised that stoicism was an overrated quality. And, far from making a woman low maintenance, all it meant in reality was a man could never relax. He would always be wondering if the bright smile actually hid an inner anguish.

Not that her anguish, inner or otherwise, was anything to do with him.

Sweat broke out like a rash over his upper lip as he relived those moments when he'd thought he wasn't going to outrun the avalanche of destruction, that he was going to see her lost under half a runaway forest.

'I suppose you think it was a brave thing to do?'

'I didn't think at all,' she admitted, punching in the hotel number and missing the anger that pulled the skin taut across the sculpted bones of his face.

Rafael could not believe this woman. She was acting as if

nothing had happened—surely she realised what danger she had been in.

He realised it.

His entire body went cold every time he realised it. Even now he could feel the fear that had clawed across his skin as he had been forced to stand by, helpless, and watch, unable to stop her until it had almost been too late.

A fine sheen of sweat broke out across the golden skin of his brow when he recalled the moment that he had thought he would not reach her in time.

He was a man who did not indulge in pointless what-if scenarios, and Rafael's knuckles stood out white on the steering wheel as he found himself unable to stop projecting images, each one more horrific than the last. They all ended the same, with her broken, crushed body, and he would have been at least indirectly responsible.

She wouldn't have been in a position to be harmed if he had not lured her away from the city. He might not have intended her actual harm, but he definitely hadn't had her best interests at heart.

If anything *had* happened to her...? The unaccustomed guilt lay heavy on Rafael's shoulders.

'They will probably inscribe that on your headstone.'

The bitterness in his voice drew Maggie's indignant gaze to his face. 'There's no need to take it out on me and I'm not planning on needing one just yet!'

Rafael, his eyes trained on the road ahead as he swerved to avoid a pothole, asked, 'Don't take what out on you?'

Maggie compressed her lips, aware that if she said she thought he had switched off the charm offensive and started to be so nasty because his expected one-night stand had turned into something more tedious it would be tantamount to an admission she had been expecting the same outcome this evening.

And you weren't?

Frowning at the ironic voice in her head, she punched in the hotel number again.

'You might as well put that phone down.'

Maggie ignored him. 'I need to leave a message.' The tour guide would not worry if she missed the optional evening entertainment, but if she didn't arrive back until the early hours it was possible that they might start to worry. 'I had plans for this evening.'

'So did I.'

She flashed him a look and he added, without looking at her, 'We have no signal here.'

'I saw you using your phone.'

An expression she struggled to interpret broke the impassive stoniness of his expression. 'There is no signal this side of the mountain.'

Despite the information, she tried once more before admitting defeat. 'What time will we reach the city?' she asked, dropping the phone back in her bag.

In the mirror he caught sight of her pressing her nose to the window like a child... Nothing else about her was childish. Recalling the softness of the warm body he had carried sent an indiscriminate pulse of lust through his body.

'You will have to delay your plans,' he informed her shortly. 'We are not going to the city.'

The abrupt afterthought sank in and Maggie swivelled in her seat. 'Is that a threat?'

He looked bored and said, 'A fact.'

'But I want—'

'What you want is not factored into my plans. You know the time—it is not practicable to drive into the city. I have a house nearby.' Beautiful women always thought the world revolved around them and just because she had a reckless streak that made her perform stupidly brave acts did not exclude Maggie Ward from this rule.

'You said you would see me safely back.'

'I did not say when.'

'So when? Next week, next month?' she enquired with silky sarcasm.

The silence stretched.

'Are you trying to scare me?'

A raw laugh left Rafael's throat. 'Scare?' How, he wondered, did you scare a woman who had so little regard for her own safety? Under that soft exterior Maggie Ward had a core of steel. 'Is it working?'

'In your dreams,' she snorted. 'Are you always this rude?'

He turned his head briefly and flashed her a grin that did not reach his steely eyes. 'Yes.'

Her jaw tightened as she angled a narrow-eyed glare of seething dislike at his profile. 'You really must be Mr Popularity.'

'People generally overlook my manners.'

'You're not *that* good-looking,' she lied, then flushed at the implied compliment.

'I'm crushed,' he said, sounding anything but.

'It shows,' she retorted, wondering how she could ever have thought this man sensitive and charming—he was a shallow, arrogant chauvinist.

'But I am that rich.'

This boast drew a scornful snort. 'I suppose you own this half of the mountain,' she said, nodding to the towering bleak presence to their left.

'And the other half and the village and two others actually.'

'And I'm a duchess. I'm not that gullible, and you're not that good a liar and as for your...*wow!*' Maggie let out a silent whistle, her gaze riveted on the illuminated façade of a stone castle complete with turrets that loomed before them.

'That is the most incredible hotel I have ever seen!' she admitted, envying the glamorous people who must stay at a place like that.

Was he planning on staying there?

If so, it was distinctly possible he hadn't been exaggerating the rich part. Well, that was one problem solved—they would have to part company. A place like that would not let her through the door looking like this.

'It is not a hotel.'

'You mean a family still lives there?' What an anachronism, she thought, in this day and age for one family to occupy so much space, but maybe seeing it sold off to a developer might be a worse crime.

Directing his car through large ornate wrought-iron gates that swished open silently at their approach, Rafael shook his head as he drove down the avenue lined with lime trees.

'No, just one person.'

'All that for one person…' She stopped, the colour receding from her already pale face as the penny finally dropped. 'It's yours, isn't it?'

CHAPTER EIGHT

HE confirmed her suspicion with a tiny nod of his head. 'You can use the landline to leave that message about your change of plans.'

'My plans haven't changed.' Maggie found herself protesting to his back.

She was presuming they were expected because as his feet hit the gravel people started to appear. Presumably, she thought sourly, to respond to the commands he was issuing—at command issuing he was definitely not an amateur.

Maggie began to struggle with the car door, her spirits slightly buoyed because she realised that all she had to do was ask the hotel to send a taxi out to pick her up.

She wasn't stranded or reliant on Rafael.

'Allow me.'

Of course the door opened smoothly for him. Maggie nodded her head in an attitude of cold courtesy. 'Thank you.' It was good to feel in control again—*you wish.*

'Can you manage or shall I carry you again?'

Was that a joke? Maggie decided she didn't want to know. She pushed away the memory of being held in his arms and waving a hand in a shooing gesture, snapped crankily, 'I've told you I'm fine.'

Catching sight of her reflection in the wing mirror, she realised that she did not look fine.

The inner masochist in her made Maggie take a second look, she barely repressed a groan.

It wasn't hard to see why the smouldering Spaniard had stopped smouldering, and who could blame him for going off her big time?

Her hair had returned to its natural curly state; surrounding her face in a dark tangled froth and hanging loose down her back, it made her look scary. As for her face minus all make-up and plus a lot of dirt... She closed her eyes and thought it was just as well the seduction idea was off the menu.

'We have mirrors inside.'

His tall figure, backlit by the light streaming through the open door, stood there, his arms folded across his exposed chest radiating impatience.

Maggie gave a grimace, embarrassed at being caught out staring at her reflection. 'I'm coming,' she huffed, jogging to catch him up.

Rafael watched her approach with a frown. 'Slow down. There's no fire.'

Maggie rolled her eyes. 'Make up your mind!' It seemed to her that it didn't really matter what she did—as far as this man was concerned it would be the wrong thing.

The massive metal-banded oak door she followed him through opened directly into what appeared to be an old banqueting hall complete with roaring fire, suits of armour and tapestries on the stone walls.

How many centuries had his family lived here? she thought, wondering what it must be like to trace your roots this far back. Her eyes widened...my God!

She spun around. 'I've forgotten your full name.'

He blinked at the confession. 'Rafael-Luis Castenadas,' he revealed, watching her face carefully for a reaction.

There was none. If she had come to search for her mother, he would have thought she would be more than familiar with the name.

'Ramon will show you where you can use the phone.'

'You…?' She was talking to his back. She wrapped her arms around her body, fighting the vulnerable sensation—vulnerable because Rafael Castenadas's presence did not offer her security.

Quite the contrary was true.

A tall thin man wearing a dark suit and a sombre expression, presumably the Ramon in question, escorted Maggie to a room off an inner hallway. Despite the massive dimensions it was actually quite cosy-looking, with book-lined walls, vibrant-coloured rugs on the polished wood floor and a fire burning in the open fireplace.

To complete the domestic picture a dog of indeterminate parentage lay asleep on one of the large sofas. It opened one eye when Maggie walked in, wagged its tail and went back to sleep.

The thin man nodded towards the phone, and went to leave.

'No…don't…' She dropped her outstretched hand when he turned.

'Can I help you?'

She gave a sigh of relief. 'Great, you speak English. I was wondering, where am I exactly…the address, I mean, of here? Does here have a name?'

If he found the request odd he did not show it, and when Maggie struggled to follow his pronunciation of the *castillo* he produced a notepad and pen from his breast pocket and wrote it down for her.

After her concern that someone might be worried, it appeared no one had noticed her absence! Maggie explained to the person at the other end that she would need a taxi to pick her up. When she gave the address, spelling it out to avoid any mistakes, there was a loud intake of breath the other end, but the hotel agreed it would be no problem.

'Oh, and how much would it be likely to cost?'

The reply to her afterthought took her breath away. 'You're joking.'

The voice the other end assured her that he was not.

Knowing that there was no way her tight holiday budget would run to that sort of money, Maggie thanked him for his trouble but explained that she'd changed her mind.

With a sigh she hung up and sat down beside the dog.

'So what,' she asked, burying her face in his fur, 'do we do now?'

She was still no nearer an answer when fifteen minutes later Rafael walked in.

He made no sound. It was the prickle on the back of her neck that made Maggie turn her head.

She stopped stroking the dog's ears.

'How long have you been standing there?' Nervous tension made her voice sharp.

He had changed and presumably showered, his wet hair was slicked back and he was wearing dark jeans and a white open-necked shirt with no tears. He could have stepped right out of a glossy page advertising...well, actually, advertising anything, because when they said that sex sold they were not wrong.

And every inch of his tall, lean, muscle-packed frame oozed sex, every hollow and plane of his dark face. Maggie's eyes drifted from the full curve of his sensual upper lip to his hooded glittering gaze and her anxiety levels went off the scale.

She licked her lips nervously and drew her knees up to her chin.

'Not long.' He clicked his fingers and the dog lifted his head, his tail thumping loudly against Maggie's legs.

Rafael said something in Spanish and the dog immediately jumped off the sofa and, tail still wagging, went and sat by his side.

'He knows he is not allowed on there, but he likes to push the boundaries…and see how far he can go.'

'Then you click your fingers and bring him to heel.' He probably used the same method with his women, she thought sourly.

And I bet it works. Imagining the sort of women a man who looked like him and lived in a place like this normally shared his bed with did not improve her mood.

Not that she had any intention of sharing his bed, even if she was invited, which now seemed doubtful. No, her loss of sanity had only been temporary she was now fully in control.

You keep telling yourself that, Maggie.

She was no longer amazed that his initial interest had waned, but she was amazed that he had ever been interested in her in the first place. She had seen the sort of woman she was willing to bet he dated, polished and elegant, not a hair out of place, not a nail chipped and not an extra inch anywhere on her svelte silhouette to ruin the line of her designer clothes.

'A reward helps,' he said as the dog took a treat from his fingers before trotting over to the fire and flopping down. 'It is sometimes hard to work out who has trained who,' he remarked ruefully.

Maggie, who couldn't imagine anyone calling him domesticated, shrugged and swept her hair across one shoulder, thinking if he resembled any animal it was a wolf.

'Sorry about your plans.' He walked across to a cabinet,

pulling out a bottle and two glasses. 'Tonight did not go as either of us anticipated.'

She laughed. 'I think you could call that the understatement of the century.' And she was betting things not going to plan was not something that happened to him often.

He didn't just have the looks and the animal magnetism, Rafael was also clearly a rich, powerful man, used to getting what he wanted.

Had he *really* wanted her…?

She breathed through the illicit thrill that raced along her nerve endings at the startling thought. The point was he was used to seeing something and getting it, and equally quickly losing interest. A car, a painting or a woman, and things went smoothly for him because people were there to make sure they went smoothly.

She was sure he had people whose sole purpose in life was to shield him from the unsightly.

Under normal circumstances their paths would never have crossed, but they had and he had thought, Why not…? Had he calculated she was worth the effort of a drive into the country, but when the effort had involved dust, tears and messy hair he had begun to regret his eccentric choice?

She tugged at the medallion that hung between her breasts and watched as he poured some amber liquid into the bottom of both glasses. 'I don't want a drink.'

He shrugged and lifted a glass to his lips. 'Well, I do.' He took the place she had vacated and looked at her over the rim of his glass; his ludicrously long, dark, spiky lashes cast a shadow along his razor-sharp cheekbones.

'Well we've both gone off the idea of a one-night stand.' She laughed and tried to act as though this were something that happened to her every day of the week. 'So where do I sleep? I'm assuming I can cadge a lift back tomorrow morning?'

She was about as convincing as silicone implants. 'You've never had a one-night stand, have you?'

Maggie considered lying, but decided it was doubtful she could pull it off. 'Not as such…' she conceded reluctantly.

A muscle beside his mouth clenched. 'But you came with me. What were you thinking of?'

Outrage with no trace of irony…talk about double standards! 'You invited me, but let me guess—it's not the same thing. God, I haven't actually been missing anything, have I? Simon probably did me a favour.' Now there was a novel thought. 'Men are a total disappointment!' she concluded heavily.

Rafael, struggling to follow the angry diatribe, picked up on one word. 'Who is Simon?'

He took a swallow of the brandy that appeared to have no effect on him, but Maggie, conscious that she was being uncharacteristically indiscreet, wondered if the effect could be passed on to her like a sympathetic pregnancy.

She was a sympathetic drunk; the frivolous imagery made her smile.

'Simon is my…was my fiancé.'

A look of utter astonishment crossed his face. 'You were engaged?'

Maggie lifted her chin. 'Why shouldn't I be engaged?' she demanded in a dangerous voice. 'What's wrong with me?' she asked, banging her chest. 'Just what's wrong with me?' Her voice stalled on a quivering note of self pity.

'Nothing is wrong with you.'

Maggie glared at his rigid blank face and snarled, 'Once more with feeling! I actually prefer you when you're incredibly rude. Mouthing polite platitudes you clearly don't believe. It's just so not you!'

'I am not rude.'

The denial made Maggie roll her eyes. 'No, you probably

call it not caring what people think. Well, newsflash, buster, it's the same thing!' she informed him, tacking on seamlessly, 'I think I will have that drink.' *Buster...?* She really had to cut down on her intake of gangster movies.

'Is that such a good idea?' he asked, wondering about the man who had let her go. Clearly not very bright, that went without saying, but what had attracted Maggie to this loser and did he still have all his limbs intact?

She might look like Angelina, but Angelina's daughter had definitely missed out on the statuesque calm gene; she was a real firebrand and bolshy with it, he thought, unable to repress the flicker of admiration.

Ignoring him, Maggie walked across to the bureau and picked up the glass. Surprised by the weight of the antique lead crystal, she weighed it in her hand before she lifted it in a silent toast. Rafael watched one brow raised, as fifty-year-old vintage brandy vanished down her throat on one gulp.

'That must have hurt.'

Maggie lifted a hand to her throat, feeling the burn all the way down to her stomach. 'It still is,' she admitted, covering her mouth politely as she coughed.

Rafael found himself laughing. He went from being furious with her to enchanted. She really was delicious and not like any woman he had ever encountered. It was as if the less she tried to please him, the more he was fascinated.

'Do they actually let you out without a keeper?'

'Time off for good, possibly *angelic* behaviour. You know what my mistake was?' The burn, she realised, had become a glow settling warmly in the pit of her stomach.

'I know I will probably regret asking this, but what was your mistake, Maggie Ward?'

'I thought I could become another person just like that.' She snapped her fingers to illustrate her point. 'But you can't... I should have started with a motorbike or a tattoo...with you I was…' She watched him shake his head in utter confusion but didn't try to explain—he'd never understand. 'You've got to keep it real and know your limits.'

Rafael, to whom *real* was fast becoming a dim and distant memory, took the half-full glass from her hand. The scary part was she was still well under the legal limit. 'And I am not real?'

'You're a mistake,' she admitted. 'Jumping in the deep end. I wanted to prove to Simon…Millie, my mum…no, *myself…*' She looked shocked by the admission and sat down abruptly. 'I really don't know what I was or am doing…a lot of things have been going on in my life just lately.' And he really wants to know this, Maggie, she admonished herself.

'Sometimes the past is better left undisturbed.' He could see how delving into a background, searching for roots, might make a person question their life.

Maggie lifted her eyes, a little bemused by the intensity of his fixed regard.

Did he think she had a past? She almost wished she did have. Either way, she wasn't about to admit she was actually a blank boring page, especially when it came to men and sex.

God, I don't want to die a virgin.

She tried to think of a suitably enigmatic response and blurted, 'But doesn't the past make us what we are?' His past had to be littered with glamorous, beautiful women.

'I like to look forward, not back.' And when he looked back on tonight, would it be with regret?

Regret that he had resisted the temptation that was driving him slowly out of his mind? Or regret because he had ignored the nagging voice of his conscience?

Did he want her so much because she was out of bounds? he speculated. And why was she out of bounds? What had changed between first seeing her and now? They were two consenting adults—why should they not enjoy each other?

'What were you thinking when I came in? You looked very deep in thought.'

'Isn't that looking backwards?'

'Touché!'

Her eyes slid of their own volition to the sensual curve of his sculpted lips.

Simon had never made her feel attractive.

The way Rafael had looked at her when they'd met, she had felt more aware of her femininity than Simon had made her feel in four years.

'You have a very impressive home.' He was a very impressive man.

'Are you changing the subject?'

'Yes.'

He released a laugh. Maggie tilted her head back as he got to his feet, and shuffled to the far end of the sofa as he sat down beside her.

'Are you feeling better?'

'Better, but a bit…' Her voice died to a whisper when he reached across and trailed a finger down her cheek. 'Near-death experiences will do that.'

She felt intense relief mingled with troubling regret when his hand fell away. 'I just keep thinking what if I hadn't met you tonight?'

Was she wondering about the confrontation with her birth mother? For the first time he considered today from Maggie's point of view.

She might have dreaded the meeting. It might have taken her weeks to work herself up to the moment and, perhaps not fully committed, still wondering if she was doing the right thing, she had stepped back.

Was she regretting it now? Was she wishing she had not allowed herself to be diverted?

'If you hadn't brought me there, would those children have…?' She shook her head.

He watched a visible shudder pass through her body and realised it was another 'what if' that was plaguing her.

'They are fine, you are fine…' A nerve in his lean jaw jerked as the slow-motion replay of the event in his head reached the moment when he had thought she would not be fine. 'You can't live your life thinking what if…' he continued hoarsely.

Maggie turned her head, their eyes meshed and Maggie felt some of the tension leave her body. She sighed slowly and nodded and said, 'But what if…?'

He loosed a husky laugh and lifted a finger to her lips. 'Enough.'

It wasn't the firm admonition that silenced Maggie, but the confusing combination of sensations that was coursing through her body.

His thumb stayed at the corner of her mouth, his eyes sealed to hers; the air was thick with an almost electrical charge that made it hard for her to breathe.

He leaned into her close, very close, but not touching. Her heavy lids half closed as she swayed closer as though drawn by some invisible thread that connected her to him. 'Your skin smells…' He exhaled and she felt his brandy-scented breath on her cheek.

He stopped and she thought, Bad…good? Say something…do something…touch me.

'It's late. We should go to bed.' He had never in his life felt a need so raw, so primal to possess a woman.

She gave a fractured sigh. Her heart rate quickened but her body relaxed. It seemed right. 'Yes.'

He met her eyes shining with promise and trust and he heard himself say, 'Perhaps this is not a good idea.'

She felt her smile slide off her face, and flinched as if he'd just thrown cold water in her face. Not water, Maggie, just a reality check. This is what happens when you start thinking you're irresistible.

She lifted her chin. 'I am a bit tired.' She gave an artistic yawn to demonstrate the point, then spoilt the pretence by adding, 'I'm not drunk, you know.'

'I know you're not.' Scruples, he decided, were very over-rated and painful, and what would be achieved by depriving them both of an experience that would, he knew, be pleasurable?

She felt the mortified heat reach her cheeks. To have one man politely excuse himself from her bed was one thing; two... There had to be something seriously wrong with her.

'This day started quite well, and this may sound dramatic but it really is turning into the worst day of my life. You'll laugh, but actually I thought...' She stopped, shook her head. He wasn't laughing; he was staring at her with a fixed intensity that she was not going to mistake for blind lust. 'I really do feel like an idiot.'

'You're not an idiot.' He took hold of her elbows and looked down into her heart-shaped face, gazing deep into her liquid dark eyes. 'But you do have a smudge on your nose...right there,' he said, kissing the spot.

Do not read anything into it, Maggie... 'It's fine—you don't fancy me...perfectly understandable...look, you're not the first man to be able to resist me. I'm not going to take it personally. I'm not really—'

'Shut up!' He hooked a finger under her chin and he captured her eyes and like a primal blast the blaze of hunger in his drove the air from Maggie's lungs in one shocked gasp.

She melted, paralysed by a combination of raw lust and desperate longing, unable to catch her breath; her fingers closed around the hard muscles of his upper arms.

'Do you want to spend the night alone, Maggie?'

Maggie's eyes closed as he kissed the corner of her mouth, her body twisting and arching as she tried to insinuate herself closer. 'No,' she whispered against his mouth. Then she opened her eyes, looked at his lean dark face so close to her own, and said, 'No!'

He smiled at the defiant declaration, a slow, predatory smile that sent her stomach into a spasm of raw excitement. The tension in the air between them thickened; it shimmered.

'Neither do I.'

CHAPTER NINE

THE raw hunger in his kiss blazed along Maggie's nerve endings, vaporising any lingering doubts or fears. This was what she wanted, Rafael was what she *needed.*

She held his face between her hands as his lips moved expertly over her own, the slow, languid exploration a torment and a revelation. At the first erotic incursion of his tongue into her moist mouth she moaned deep in her throat and opened her mouth to invite him deeper, meeting his tongue with her own.

They kissed with a frantic hunger and all the time he touched her, his hands sliding over her soft womanly curves, dragging moans from her lips.

When he did lift his mouth fractionally from hers it was to rasp, 'I love your mouth. It is a miracle. You are a miracle...so soft.' He ran a finger down her throat, his eyes darkening as he felt the deep shiver that rippled through her body. 'So sensitive to my touch.'

'You won't stop, will you?'

She felt the rumble of laughter vibrate in his chest as he pulled her under him and laid her full length on the sofa. There was no laughter in his face as he stared down at her, just a fierce, relentless hunger that tightened the knot of excitement low in her belly.

'Not any time soon,' he promised huskily as he lowered his body onto hers. 'I don't believe any man could resist you. It is not possible… *Madre mia,* I have wanted you from the moment I saw you.'

Maggie gasped, her eyes flying wide as she felt the pressure of his arousal against her belly. Her arms slid around his middle, pulling him closer. She was revelling in the amazing feel of his lean hard body against her and pleasurably conscious of the fresh rush of liquid heat between her thighs.

The heat burned between them as they kissed, he touched her everywhere. Maggie slid her hands under the hem of his shirt. She heard him gasp at the touch of her fingers on his bare flesh and would have pulled her hand away but he caught her wrist and, holding her eyes, placed it back on his body, spreading her fingers and saying huskily, 'I want to feel your hands on me, *querida.'*

Maggie's throat was too congested with emotion to speak. She nodded mutely and trailed her fingers slowly across the ridges of muscle on his flat belly.

Rafael closed his eyes, sucked in a breath, then lowered his head and kissed her with a driving ferocity that made her head swim. His mouth still connected to hers, he raised himself off her, unfastened his shirt with one hand and stroked her face with the other, his fingers tangled in her hair.

Maggie opened her eyes just as the fabric parted. Weak with lust and longing she stared, her passion-glazed stare moving hungrily over the gleaming hard lines of his grey-hound-lean, muscle-ridged bronze torso.

A deep, sobbing moan was wrenched from her throat. The sound made the hairs on the nape of Rafael's neck stand on end and propelled him into frenzied action.

Slowed only by the tremor in his fingers, he unbuckled his belt and slid his jeans over his hips before kicking them away.

Kneeling astride her, clad only in boxers—the erotic image,

she knew, would be permanently etched in her brain—he began to undress her.

Every brush of his fingers on her hot skin sent shimmies of tingling sensation along her sensitised nerve endings.

As he peeled her bra from her shoulders a deep gasp was wrenched from deep in the vault of Rafael's chest. His golden skin glistened with the need that drove him as he stripped off her pants, sliding them with tantalising slowness over her smooth thighs.

Suddenly overwhelmed by self-consciousness she gasped, 'This isn't me!' And tried to cover herself.

Rafael caught her hands and pinned them above her head, holding them lightly there with his hand.

'Look at me.'

Maggie reluctantly turned her head. Without a shred of self-consciousness he divested himself of the boxers she had imagined concealed nothing; it turned out they did. She swallowed and felt her cheeks burn as guiltily she wrenched her eyes higher.

'This is me, and you are allowed to look, and want and touch. There is no shame, just sex. This is natural and good.' He had a very poor opinion of the person who had made her feel differently. 'This *is* you...and I will look. I will look because you are—' he swallowed as his glance dropped '—*Dios mio,* your are perfect...so unbelievably perfect.'

He cupped one pink-tipped breast in his hand, drawing the straining point between his fingers, rubbing the sensitised flesh before he lowered his head and applied his tongue to the engorged nub.

Maggie writhed under his touch, her fingers sinking deep into his hair. Her hips lifted as he ran his tongue down the soft curve of her belly, then lower.

As he parted the delicate folds, stroking her, Maggie

squeezed her eyes tight closed and cried his name over and over until she could bear no more.

'This is...please...'

Satisfied that he had brought her to the brink and barely able to control his own driving hunger, Rafael settled between her parted thighs.

His hot, hungry eyes broke through the last shreds of Maggie's shredded control. Face flushed, dark velvet eyes glazed with passion, she spread her thighs wider and, reaching for him, whispered, 'Please, I need you inside...'

And then amazingly he was and she had not come close to imagining how impossibly marvellous, how *incredible* it could feel to have him throbbing hard and hot, filling her.

He registered her incredible tightness and her cry as he entered her and it took a few seconds for his brain to link the two and produce the explanation.

Her body tightened around him and Rafael could no longer resist the temptation to sink deeper into her silky smoothness.

Maggie's legs wrapped around his hips. It was incredible. She kissed his chest and hung on as each thrust of his body sent her deeper into a blissful delirium.

Above her his face was a rigid mask as he struggled to control himself to give her a taste of the pleasure she had never experienced.

When it hit her, the first wave of orgasm shocked a fractured cry from Maggie. Her head went back and she clung to him as another and another hit her, then exploded into a deep pulse of pleasure that went all the way to her toes... As the wave receded she felt Rafael stiffen above her and shiver as the heat of his release filled her.

Holding her head against his chest, Rafael stroked her dark hair. Their bodies slowly cooled. Maggie lay listening to the beat of his heart slow before she lifted her head and smiled at him.

Rafael did not smile back. He didn't say a word. He just lifted her up and, draping a throw around them both, carried her from the room and through the silent maze of hallways into a room that was dominated by a large four-poster bed.

He didn't take her to the bed. Instead he walked into the adjoining bathroom, a massive room of startling decadence with a vast sunken marble bath, armchairs and a carved fireplace with candles set in the grate and along the mantle.

With her in his arms he walked straight into the walk-in shower and switched on the water. As she watched the spray run over his dark face, making his skin glisten, he set Maggie on her feet.

Then still without a word he took the citrus-scented gel from an applicator and began to lather her skin. Gently but thoroughly he washed her, moving his hand in firm circular motions until she tingled everywhere.

Maggie didn't break the silence she just stood passively, her throat constricted by a myriad conflicting emotions she didn't want to analyse. The warm water was soothing, easing the aches and bruises on her body.

There was nothing remotely sexual about his ministrations, even though she could hardly *not* notice the fact that he was aroused.

It was all a little surreal. She felt as though she were watching the scene from outside her body, and strangely the experience was on one level even more intimate than what had preceded it.

Finally he switched off the water. He carefully wrung the excess moisture from her hair and swathed her in a towel, using another to dry her from head to toe before picking her up once more and striding back into the bedroom. The fire in this room was lit. Flames crackled as he pulled back the covers on the bed and laid her naked body on the crisp sheets.

She watched as Rafael used the damp towel to cursorily

blot the moisture on his own body before climbing in beside her.

He pulled her to him, fitting her curves into his angles before tilting her face up to his.

Finally he broke his silence.

'Now, *querida,* we will do this thing the way it should be done.'

'I thought it was fine the first time,' she admitted, feeling so relaxed that she was boneless, though sexual awareness remained like a prickle under her skin.

He kissed the pulse spot at the base of her slender neck and the prickle became an itch.

'You are not a woman who should settle for "fine" and I am not a man who delivers it.'

He delivered this not as an arrogant boast but more in the form of a simple statement of fact, and Maggie accepted it as such. When it came to matters carnal she was quite prepared to accept that Rafael was the expert.

'But?'

He touched a finger to her lips. 'And afterwards we will discuss how it is that you were a virgin.' His eyes darkened; the discovery was one that would stay with him for ever. 'I could have hurt you and that would have…'

The expression of self-loathing on his face as he broke off and swallowed hard drew a cry of protest from Maggie. 'You didn't—you were perfect.'

His mouth curved into a complacent smile. 'Yes, you mentioned that. Don't blush—a man likes to be appreciated.' The smile faded from his face. 'Now let me show you how much I appreciate you.'

Maggie's eyes darkened. 'Please,' she whispered.

Much later as he lay still sheathed in the heat between her thighs Rafael struggled to make sense of his reluctance to break the physical connection even though his sexual hunger and hers were satisfied—finally.

He looked at her face pressed against the curve of his shoulder her lashes dark on her cheek as she surrendered to sleep and he realised it was foolish to analyse such things. It was not as if it were a meeting of souls; they were sexually compatible. Maggie was an amazingly passionate woman and an incredibly intuitive lover.

Rafael suspected there was still more passion there just waiting to be awakened. It was a pity that she would not be here long enough for him to unlock that promise.

CHAPTER TEN

MAGGIE put down her coffee cup and stared at Rafael. She waited for the maid who had fetched fresh coffee to leave before she replied to his invitation.

'You're suggesting I spend the rest of my holiday here, with you.'

Rafael refilled his own cup. 'It seems logical.'

His idea of logic and hers were very different. 'Not logical—mad.'

'How so?'

She looked at him in astonishment. 'It's totally crazy.'

'That is not an argument and, anyway,' he said, considering her freshly scrubbed image with a smile, 'I think you need some crazy in your life.'

She shook her head. 'Last night was enough crazy to last me a lifetime.'

'I seriously doubt that.' He planted his elbows on the table and leaned towards her, a knowing look on his face. 'You're thinking about it, aren't you?'

She responded to the goad with a frown and firm denial that she almost immediately cancelled by saying, 'I couldn't?'

'But you want to.'

'I have plans.'

Rafael, who knew about her plans, said, 'Dump your plans.'

She tried to look amused when she asked, 'Do women always dump their plans for you?' Because of course she knew they did and she knew why.

Last night had been the most mind-blowing experience of Maggie's life, and she would cherish it forever. Walking away this morning was hard—in a week's time just how much harder would it be?

The thought frightened her and made her hesitate.

'You will not regret it, I promise.' While she was here with him Angelina was safe.

You're such a saint.

Rafael ignored the sardonic voice in his head and added, 'Did I not fulfil my promises last night?'

Maggie closed her eyes, hearing his smoky voice in her head promising her a glimpse of paradise and more. And he had made good on the promises more than once.

'I've got nothing here, no clothes…no…'

He glanced at the watch on his wrist. 'I am having your luggage brought from the hotel. It should be here shortly.'

Maggie laughed. 'You were that sure I'd stay?'

'I was that sure that I want you to stay. I will make this a holiday to remember.'

'It's already that.' It would be strange going back to her normal life after this.

'So why do you look sad?' He had never experienced a desire to make a woman smile before, but he did now.

She shook her head. 'I'm not sad…mad possibly,' she conceded, 'but not sad, just…' She screwed up her nose and gazed around the room. 'This is not my life.'

'What is your life?' Rafael heard himself ask and frowned. This situation had been a lot simpler when he had thought of her as a problem to be solved. When, he wondered, had she become a person?

A beautiful and desirable person, and her smile made him happy.

The question seemed serious. She stared at him and then to lessen the intensity of the moment she summoned a smile. 'If you have a spare five minutes I might actually take you up on that invitation. But seriously…'

He cut across her. 'I was being serious.'

Her eyes fell from his. His intensity was unsettling; actually, he was unsettling.

She gave a strained little laugh. 'I'm sure you're not really interested…'

'I asked, didn't I?'

'I work in a city casualty unit. I'm a nurse.'

'A nurse?'

She tilted her head to one side and studied his face. 'You sound surprised.'

'I am,' he admitted, though now he thought about it he could see her in the role. 'The last time I was in a casualty department in England my nurse was a rugby player called Tomas. I'm feeling cheated.'

The glow in his eyes made her dizzy and excited.

'So its not just last night—you spend your time saving lives.'

Maggie gave an embarrassed shrug. 'It's not normally so dramatic and there is no danger involved, except of course when a drunk decides to take a swing.'

Rafael tensed. 'At you?'

Maggie who couldn't stop staring at the muscles clenching and unclenching beside his mouth, nodded. 'It has been known,' she admitted, blinking as he loosed a stream of fluid, angry-sounding Spanish. 'Don't worry,' she added, patting the clenched hand that lay nearest her and saying cheerily, 'I can take care of myself and I have very quick reflexes.'

'What sort of world are we living in when a nurse takes being assaulted for granted? *Madre di Dio,* your family allow this?' he grated incredulously.

'It's not really a question of allowing, is it? I'm over eighteen…I'm over twenty-one, and I've never been assaulted. It happens, but not to me.'

'But it could. Well, I,' he announced autocratically, 'would not permit it.'

'Well, I'm glad I'm not your sister.'

'So am I, but I have no sister.'

'Your father and mother?' she asked, wondering about this man whom she was alone with and realising he had told her nothing about himself. She had slept with a stranger and she had agreed to stay with him.

His shoulders lifted in a shrug. 'Both dead.'

The pragmatic statement did not invite sympathy but Maggie's tender heart ached. 'I can't imagine what that would be like.' A shadow crossed her face as she imagined a life that did not contain her family.

'So you have a family…?' Having pushed the Angelina question to the back of his mind, he did not enjoy the topic being front and centre where he could not ignore it.

She reached into her bag and pulled a family snapshot she always carried from her wallet. She held out her hand and offered it to him.

Maggie frowned as she watched an expression of astonishment wash over his dark face. He was looking at the snapshot as if it were an alien.

'Is something wrong? You don't have to—' She began to withdraw her hand but he caught her wrist.

'No, nothing's wrong,' he promised, taking the photo, not

because he actually felt any interest but because he knew it would have injured her feelings if he had refused.

Feelings were entirely new territory for him and he saw no urgent need to explore this development.

'I'm more used to being offered bills for designer shoes.'

Her brow furrowed in confusion at the comment. 'Why? Do you have a business interest?'

He regarded her in much the same way she imagined he might had she just announced that she believed in Santa Claus.

'No, I have girlfriends with expensive tastes who like me to pick up the tab.' He did not begrudge the expense, he considered himself a generous lover.

The plural was not wasted on Maggie.

Good God, where is your pride, Maggie?

I'm sleeping with a man who, not only does not promise something as basic as exclusivity, he probably doesn't understand the meaning of the word.

'If you ever pay for my shoes I will feed them to you.'

He stared. 'You don't like shoes?'

'You may not mind women who sleep with you for your money, but I mind being mistaken for one.' She pinned him with a wrathful glare and yelled, 'I'm sleeping with you for the sex! On a temporary basis, obviously.'

'Obviously, and I promise not to offend you with shoes, though I would like to point out that I like to think it is not just my money they sleep with me for.'

Maggie's eyes narrowed. She knew they didn't and she hated them all with a vengeance. 'You really do love yourself!'

His lashes lifted from his cheek and he levelled a direct look into her eyes. 'Love is not something I encourage.'

Maggie blinked. The warning was unmistakeable. Then before she could respond to it he began to study the snapshot, saying, 'Those are your brothers?' The young men in the slightly out of focus snapshot were both blond and broad-shouldered and duplicates of their father. All three men towered over their sister, and the woman in the wheelchair.

She nodded, wishing she had remembered sooner that this was not the most flattering photo she had ever appeared in. 'I still had my braces then.'

'Which accounts for the lack of a smile? The woman in the wheelchair…your mother?'

'Yes.' Maggie did not want to go into details, but added, 'But she's not in the wheelchair any more—at least, not all the time.'

'Your brothers are not much like you.'

Maggie grinned. Talking about her family made this abnormal situation seem less surreal. 'You mean because they're six feet four or because they're blond?' she suggested, raising a hand to her dark hair and grimacing as she realised it had come free of the ponytail and now hung loose in a tangled skein down her back.

'Your colouring is very…Mediterranean?' His glance moved across the glowing contours of her face. Her skin was flawless and had a peachy sheen that was almost opalescent. The idea of carrying her back to bed became more urgent than eating breakfast.

Maggie's eyes fell evasively, her long lashes brushing the soft curve of her smooth high cheekbones, but not before Rafael had seen the emotion flicker across her face.

'Actually, I wouldn't look like Ben and Sam. I'm adopted.'

'That must have been a shock…discovering you're adopted.' Rafael suggested, watching her push the gleaming strands of hair back from her heart-shaped face with both hands, looping it into a heavy bunch before letting it fall down her back.

She shook her head. 'Not really. I didn't *discover*—I

always knew I was adopted. Mum and Dad always made me feel special because they picked me.'

'But your brothers, they are...?'

'Big surprises, with an emphasis on the big,' she added with an affectionate grin. She felt some of the tension slip from her shoulders as a mental picture of her younger siblings formed in her head. 'Mum and Dad thought they couldn't have children so they were pretty shocked when Ben came along and then, a year later, Sam.'

'So your real mother?' he probed, wary of pushing too hard.

Her smile vanished. 'Let's talk about something else,' she suggested.

Rafael gave a casual shrug and didn't push.

'I really envy you being bilingual... Spanish is such a marvellous language and you have an incredible home. I have never met anyone who lived in a castle before.' She stopped, drew breath, and prayed for the floor to open and swallow her.

She had just taken inane babble to an entirely new level. On the plus side, at least she had run out of breath before she asked him about his heating bills!

No, actually there was no plus side.

'We don't have to talk at all.'

The invitation in his smoky, sinfully sexy voice would have been obvious no matter what language he chose to use. Maggie's breath snagged in her throat. Her eyes fused with his and Maggie's insides melted.

She reached for the coffee pot and refilled her cup. 'This is great coffee,' she enthused.

'Or we could...?' Rafael conceded drily.

Maggie, who couldn't stop staring at his long tapering fingers—she had never looked at a man's hands and thought about them on her skin, but now she had she couldn't stop— blurted with incurable honesty, 'I feel very out of my depth.'

She levelled her candid gaze at his face and wondered how she had ever been mad enough to think a one-night stand with him was a good idea.

'Once you learn to tread water, depth is not a problem.'

'I can't swim.'

'But you are a very fast learner.'

She blushed and looked at him through her lashes. 'You're a passable teacher, but you're also the sort of man I'd normally cross the road to avoid. You're not my type at all. It's crazy, but from the moment I saw you I…'

'You what?'

Maggie shivered. He had a voice that was the auditory equivalent of having your skin stroked against the deep pile of rich velvet.

'The moment I saw you I wondered…I wondered what sort of kisser you were.' And you had to tell him that why, exactly?

Rafael didn't move, didn't blink, but she heard the breath leave his lungs in one audible hiss.

She carried on looking at him.

It was said and there was no way she could unsay it. Near-death experiences did not make you braver, they clearly made you more stupid!

'God, pretend I didn't say that. I'm embarrassing myself…' she admitted, not looking at him. 'I'm embarrassing you.'

'I am not easy to embarrass.'

Her eyes lifted. 'I know,' she conceded unable to take her eyes off his dark face. 'Not that I'm suggesting that's a bad thing. It wasn't a criticism,' she added hastily, thinking not many people looking at his face would find much to criticise.

Her embarrassed little laugh transmuted into a sharp intake of breath as he left the table and came round to join her.

Holding her eyes, he took her hand and drew her up to him. Placing a hand behind her head, he tilted her face up to him.

'I too wondered when I saw you how you would taste. I wanted to find out right there in the street.' And what man would not? How could any man with red blood in his veins resist the combination of warm sexuality, wide-eyed innocence and a body made for pleasure? 'What would you have done if I had?'

'Screamed, called for help...?' she suggested, struggling to inject amusement into her voice and failing totally—her breath was coming in short choppy spurts that made it difficult to breath and impossible to raise her voice above a whisper.

'And now?' he asked, running his thumb across the cushiony pink surface of her lips.

She closed her eyes because looking at the flame burning deep in his—a trick of the light, probably—made her dizzy, and said, 'Are you going to kiss me or torture me?' She held her arms wide in a come and get me gesture and, eyes still tight shut, tilted her head back in invitation.

'When you put it like that I see it would be an act of charity to put you out of your misery.' The fever in his blood as he looked down at her made him shake—literally shake with need.

She tensed in anticipation of the plundering pressure of his lips; the light touch on the corner of her mouth took her by surprise.

Maggie's eyes flickered open. They were still open, welded to the silver gleam in his, as he increased the pressure slightly as his tongue followed the curve of her mouth, leaving a damp trail.

The heat and frustration inside Maggie mounted as she noticed just how ragged her breathing was.

'How was that for you?'

'You know your way around a mouth. Thank you.'

'Don't thank me yet,' he breathed against her mouth.

So I would get a good score, hmm?

His wicked grin flashed as he took her face between his big hands.

'That was not a kiss, that was merely the beginning... foreplay. I love the way you blush...I love your skin...'

'There is only so much foreplay, Rafael, a girl can take.'

The touch of his warm lips as they claimed her sent a tide of heat through her body. Rafael's arms slid around her body, pulling her close into him. Maggie's arms curled around his neck as she raised herself up on tiptoe and leaned into the male hardness of his lean body, excited by the leashed hunger that made him shake.

The excitement spiralled at the first sensual stab of his tongue into the warm, moist recesses of her mouth. She moaned with need and kissed him back, her hands bunching into fists as she grabbed the fabric of his shirt.

'I'm so sorry, darling, I had no idea.'

Maggie jumped away from him as if shot. Blinking as she struggled to clear the sexual fog in her brain, she stared. For some reason the star of a top American detective series was standing in the doorway.

CHAPTER ELEVEN

In the flesh and without the benefit of lighting and make-up and minus the skin-hugging trademark leather trousers Camilla Davenport was even more beautiful than the wise-cracking detective she played on the small screen.

Five ten in her bare feet, which she wasn't—her heels had to be at least four inches—she was dressed in what was probably the latest fashion. It was hard to find fault.

And Maggie tried!

In real life the actress's eyes were actually bluer, her lips even more incredibly pouty, and her breasts—was it even possible—more perky. And the people who said the camera put on ten pounds were obviously lying.

Was he sleeping with her?

Of course he was sleeping with her.

Maggie felt sick and stupid and plain. A plain, stupid woman throwing up—that would leave a great lasting impression, because obviously she was leaving. It would save him the bother of asking her to go.

'Camilla, what are you doing here?'

Rafael dragged a not quite steady hand through his dark hair and turned a less than welcoming glare on his ex-lover.

'And how did you get past Security?'

'Oh, don't blame them—nobody told the darlings I am yes-

terday's news. Rafe, *darling*, you look absolutely scrummy…'
She advanced with a purposeful sexy sway and kissed him on
the cheek, not from intention, but because he turned his head
before she landed the kiss.

She gave a sigh and stroked a red-painted nail down his
cheek. 'As always,' she said, adding with a pout, 'you are a
spoilsport.'

Rafael issued her a glare of seething impatience and her
hand fell away.

'Oh, all right, look, I can see my timing is absolutely lousy
as usual—' she flashed Maggie a friendly look apparently
totally all right to find her lover with another woman '—but
I was up here to check on the house. I'm thinking of putting
in a new pool. I have a little villa just across the valley,' she
explained to Maggie. 'Rafael makes a *very* friendly neigh-
bour.'

'I can imagine,' Maggie said, trying hard not to, but
Camilla's attention and her fluttering eyelashes had already
returned to Rafael.

'So I thought I'd come and say sorry in person and I am
truly…'

Rafael struggled to contain his impatience. 'For what?'

She widened her eyes in amazement. 'God, you don't
know! Wow, that's…awkward.' She lifted her brows and
grimaced in Maggie's direction. 'He always reads the papers
from cover to cover, doesn't he? But not today. I guess he was
busy.'

Maggie blushed and Camilla gave a husky laugh and said,
'You're different.' Her attention swung back to Rafael. 'All
right, I'll come clean. You remember that gorgeous weekend
we spent on your yacht?'

'I remember.'

Would anyone notice if she slipped out? Maggie wondered
bitterly. Or on second thought she might make a scene, a big,

noisy scene, and smash a few things because dignity was not, in her opinion, any substitute for broken crockery.

Different—presumably that translated as not glamorous.

Camilla took a folded newspaper from her bag and spread it on the table. Rafael, oblivious to Maggie's violent plans, did not even glance at it.

He can't even take his eyes off the woman, Maggie thought miserably…and who can blame him?

'That afternoon on the deck when we got… It turns out we weren't alone. Tragic, I know, and so shocking—there's absolutely no privacy these days. I think it must have been that speedboat that passed…'

'Just as you took off your top.'

Maggie closed her eyes and thought, Just kill me now, let me die or, failing that, let me come up with a really good exit line!

'Timing is everything.'

Rafael walked over to Maggie's side. She tensed as she felt his fingers massage the tense muscles of her neck. 'You all right?'

Maggie moved away and, unable to come up with an exit line of any variety, mumbled, 'No, if you'll excuse me…'

He moved to block her exit and declared autocratically, 'No, I won't. I want you to hear this.'

Tears of anger and humiliation formed in her eyes. Did he want to rub her nose in it for some reason, or was he genuinely unaware of how humiliating this was for her?

Maggie wasn't sure which explanation was the worst.

'So why are these photos appearing now, Cami, three months after the event?'

Cami and *Rafe?* She really wanted to throw up now. A choked sound escaped Maggie's throat.

'What's wrong?'

That he could ask the question spoke volumes about his sheer titanic insensitivity.

'I always knew there was something missing, now I know what it is…a pet name for you, *darling*.'

The corners of Rafael's mouth twitched. 'I'm sure you'll think of something, *honeybunch*.' He turned back to the other woman and folded his arms across his chest. The levity left his eyes as he snapped coldly, 'Come clean, Cami.'

'All right, I can see you've guessed—you always do. The studio are meeting this weekend and there have been rumours flying around that they are going to cancel the show. The viewing figures were low, but that was because they killed off my love interest…I always said—'

'Cami!'

'All right, all right. I arranged for the photo to be taken as an insurance policy, and it turned out I needed it, and,' she added, clapping her hands and releasing a squeal of delight, 'it has worked. The photos are all over the Internet, your name guarantees that, and the studio have been on the phone all morning. They are *definitely* going to commission a third series and give me a pay hike. Aren't I brilliant?'

Rafael was at his most dry as he responded, 'Not the word I would have used.'

Cami gave a wide complacent smile. 'I knew you wouldn't be mad if I explained things.'

'You are a very devious woman, Cami.'

Maggie had struggled to follow the explanation—the American spoke very quickly and her brain was on a go-slow—but if she had got the facts even half right Rafael's attitude made no sense. The woman had used him and the apparent public appetite for stories about him, and he didn't even seem mad.

That made no sense at all unless…unless he was in love with the beautiful actress.

'Darling, a girl has to watch her back in this business if she doesn't have a man to do it for her.'

'Your agent would sell his soul for you, always supposing he ever had one.'

'Gus is a treasure but he doesn't do it for free.' She picked up a croissant from the table. 'You know, I'm totally starving.'

Rafael put his hands on her shoulders and turned her around. 'Say goodbye, Cami.'

She gave a philosophical smile. 'Goodbye...' She waved over her shoulder to Maggie, who stood like a small statue and watched Rafael steer her through the door.

When he returned a few moments later she was still standing in exactly the same place.

'Your luggage has arrived,' he said, setting her cases on the floor.

Maggie expelled a deep shuddering sigh and felt the life return to her body, and the anger and the burning humiliation.

She marched over to him and picked them up. 'I won't be unpacking.'

'Fine. I will buy you new clothes.'

She scrunched up her face in a grimace of loathing. 'I would prefer to walk around naked!' she yelled.

'I can work with that.'

She compressed her full lips into a thin line. 'I have no interest in being part of your harem!'

He studied her angry face for a moment in silence. 'Do you not think that perhaps you are overreacting?' he suggested calmly.

'Mildly!'

She stood her ground as he walked across to her, though by the time he reached her side her knees were shaking.

'You're crying.'

'Not because I give a damn about your sleazy sex life, I'm mad, that's all.'

'You're jealous.' The first display of jealousy was his signal to walk, but Rafael could see that this situation was different.

In what way exactly? asked the pedantic voice in his head.

Different required a different approach—not compromise, because he did not do compromise, but an explanation perhaps?

'You have no cause. Cami and I were lovers...'

She rolled her eyes. 'Shock, horror, call the press—oh, I forgot,' she trilled. 'They already know.' The world knows and he appears to care less. 'And save your explanations. I'm just someone you picked up—you don't owe me any.'

'Do not speak of yourself in that manner!' There was a reason he had spent his life facing problems head-on and not manipulating and nice talking his way around them—nice talk didn't work!

She blinked at the lash of anger in his voice.

'It's the truth.'

'It is a crude version of the truth and you are deliberately trying to provoke me.' A spasm of impatience tightened his lean face as he snapped, 'Shut up and listen. Past tense—we were lovers. I do not have a harem, I have one lover in my bed at a time and at the moment it is you.' And for some reason even though she drove him insane he wanted it to stay that way.

'You're not sleeping with anyone else.'

'I do not make a habit of explaining myself to people.' So what was he doing now?

'All right, you may not be sleeping with her, but you wish you were. It's obvious. You weren't even angry with her and she used you.'

'That was always a possibility.'

The calm admission made her stare.

'Cami is without scruples—charming,' he conceded, 'but utterly self-centred.'

'And good in bed,' Maggie, slightly mollified by his scathing assessment, inserted with a sniff.

He did not deny it, but no matter how expert a lover he had taken he had always been conscious of an empty, knowing sense of dissatisfaction even after the most satisfactory sex.

The feeling had been absent last night and this morning. Possibly her inexperience added a challenge that he needed?

'There are a hundred Camis—a thousand. I meet them wherever I go.' He studied the tear-stained face turned up to his and wondered if he would ever meet a Maggie again.

As she watched him dismiss the actress with a click of his long fingers she wondered if he would dismiss her in the near future in a similar fashion. He almost certainly would and the knowledge gave her a horrid sinking feeling in the pit of her stomach.

'Look, I could lock myself away behind high walls and massive security and never have an unflattering photo of me snapped. But I consider the price too high.'

'But you have a lot of money.'

The observation drew a grim smile from Rafael. 'It is not a question of cost.'

'Something only a very rich person would say.'

Rafael ignored her wry interjection and said quietly, 'I would become a virtual prisoner. Instead I walk the middle ground. I do not actively seek publicity and on occasions I go out of my way to avoid it, but I do not lose sleep over every insane story that appears about me.'

Maggie frowned, considering his words. 'All right.'

He regarded her warily. 'I believe you and I might have overreacted slightly.' *Slightly!* She had broken out with a bad case of the green monster; the amazing thing was he hadn't run for the hills.

'So we can go back to where we were before the interruption?'

The sultry look she flashed him through her lashes sent a pulse of lust through his already aroused body. 'I think we'd got past the foreplay.'

'Do not be so impatient,' he charged, slipping his hands around her waist. It was so tiny that he could almost span it. 'I am still waiting for you to score me on my kisses.' He pressed an open-mouth kiss to her neck and her head fell bonelessly back. 'Be generous,' he pleaded huskily.

CHAPTER TWELVE

MAGGIE forced her heavy eyelids open. Rafael's face was so close she could see the gold tips on his lashes and feel the warmth of his breath on her cheek. 'I'm thinking possibly above average.'

He inclined his dark head fractionally without taking his eyes from hers. 'Thank you.'

'You're welcome,' she said, breathing in his warm male musky scent and feeling dizzy—in a good way.

'You're a very beautiful woman.' He slid a hand into her hair and let the silky strands run through his fingers. 'A sensual woman.'

'You really think so?'

The indentation between his brows deepened. 'If you have any doubts, then I've been doing something wrong.'

'No, Rafael, you do everything right…so right it hurts…' She pressed a hand low on her stomach to show him where her agony was centred.

His smouldering eyes slipped to her mouth. Very slowly he lowered his head and kissed her; he kissed as if he would drain her, then he lifted her up into his arms and strode from the room.

'You do know all this macho stuff does nothing for me,'

she said, teasing the sensitive skin behind his ear with her flickering tongue.

'You are very bad for my ego.'

'Well, you're incredibly good for mine,' she confessed struggling even now to get her head around the fact the marvellous man fancied the socks off her.

Rafael removed more than her socks and she enjoyed every single second of it. She was determined to savour every moment of their short time together.

Over the next few days Maggie did not lose sight of her vow.

She did indeed extract the last ounce of pleasure from everything, from the sound of his laughter, to waking and feeling the warm weight of his arm across her waist, and the intimacy of a candlelit meal and a shared bottle of wine.

She savoured everything and firmly pushed away the lurking knowledge that it would all shortly end. It was getting harder to ignore the ticking clock.

She woke on the Wednesday and thought, Two days left.

She opened her eyes and the cheerless thought slipped away. Rafael's head was on the pillow beside her, his long lashes lying in dark fans across the chiselled contours of his cheekbones, his jaw darkened with a layer of piratical dark stubble.

Sleep had ironed some of the severity from his patrician features and the hank of dark hair flopping across his high forehead made him look younger.

She could have carried on looking at his face for ever.

Over the days some of his defences had come down and he had opened up and spoken to her about his family and the uncomfortable relationship he had had with his father, who sounded to Maggie like a sadistic monster.

When Maggie had voiced her opinion he had laughed, and told her that his father had never been that interesting.

She had learnt about his mother more slowly. Sometimes she had caught a look of surprise on his face when he'd spoken of her. She got the impression that it was not something he did often.

Then the previous night as they had lain, their bodies still cooling in the aftermath of lovemaking so intense that it had made her weep, he had explained abruptly why he had reacted so strongly to her tears.

'I was ten when my mother left. I never saw her again. She was crying.'

The association, it seemed, had stayed with him always.

He had not revealed the story in one go, it had slipped out in fragments that Maggie had joined like a puzzle to see the big picture, and it was a very sad picture that had made her tender heart ache for him. Though, knowing how allergic he was to any form of sympathy, she had made her response practical, contenting herself with hugging him hard until he'd laughingly asked if she was trying to break his ribs.

Amazingly he was not bitter that when faced with the stark choice his mother had chosen her lover over her son. He was not even sorry she had left, because, he'd explained, her marriage was killing her.

Maggie had realised that he wasn't speaking metaphorically.

She had fought back tears as he'd described watching her being reduced to a shadow of herself by her destructive marriage.

Aching with empathy, Maggie had felt his frustration—a child who had had to stand by and watch helplessly the systematic destruction of someone he loved.

No, it seemed that the thing that haunted Rafael was the angry words he had yelled at her while she left. Things he had never been able to retract because she and her lover had died not long afterwards in a train smash.

Maggie, her tender heart bleeding for the vulnerable child he had been, had wrapped her arms tight around him, laying her head on his warm chest.

'She would have known you didn't mean it. She must have known you loved her. And the last thing she'd want is for you to carry on beating yourself up over it. I mean, *she* must have been eaten up with guilt.'

She wasn't sure if her comments had helped but she hoped so. It had been late before they had slept and, not wanting to wake him now, she slipped from their bed careful not to disturb him. Shrugging on a towelling gown, she went downstairs to the big kitchen where she helped herself to coffee from the fresh pot on the stove before pulling a warm roll from the basket. Tossing it from one hand to the other as it burnt her fingers, she reached for a plate and the butter.

She was topping the butter with jam when Ramon entered the kitchen looking uncharacteristically flustered.

'If you're looking for him, the boss is still asleep.'

She hesitated to add, 'Can I help?' because, although the staff rather surprisingly acted as though her position in the household were permanent and had developed a habit of consulting her on domestic issues, Maggie was very conscious of her temporary status and always referred them to Rafael, who was not always appreciative of her tact. Only the previous day he had become extremely exasperated and referred the problem back to her after she had refused to mediate a minor domestic dispute.

'That is the problem. Sabina took it on herself to wake him when the guests—'

'He has guests?' Maggie tightened her robe.

This was the first time the outside world had intruded on her little idyll and it was an unwelcome reminder of how flimsy the foundations her happiness was based on actually were.

The world was out there and, like it or not, she had to go

back into it. She had wondered what she would say if Rafael suggested continuing their relationship after her holiday ended.

She had agonised over her response, finding the thought of never seeing him again hard to contemplate without horror. But would drifting slowly apart, as they inevitably would, be less painful? A cancelled visit, a missed call, watching the gradual disintegration of their relationship? Wouldn't a clean break be easier in the long run to bear?

In the end the question might be academic; he might not suggest it. While he never mentioned it ending, he never mentioned it carrying on either. And Rafael had never given any indication that he considered their time together anything other than a pleasant interlude.

For her part Maggie had resisted it, but she had finally been forced to ask herself why when she was around him her heart reacted independently of her brain.

He was the love of her life, and though she had always scoffed at the better-to-have-loved-and-lost theory she would not have had it any other way.

Him not returning her love was a tragedy, but not ever meeting him would in her mind have been an even greater one. She had embarked on the affair thinking that sex might liberate; in reality love had.

'I think I'll take my coffee upstairs.'

'Well, if you think that…' Ramon stopped. 'Perhaps that might be best, but I thought…' He shook his head and vanished, leaving Maggie to stare after him in perplexed bemusement.

The reason for his stress became more obvious when she entered the grand hall, her intention to take the short cut up the main staircase to their room.

She came to a halt and tried to blend into the background. Rafael was standing at the far end in the company of a man and woman, who was pushing a pram up and down with her foot.

The raised angry voices of the two men made it clear she had wandered into the middle of a private argument. Unsure whether to retrace her steps and use one of the rear staircases or try and slip unnoticed up this one, she hesitated uncertainly.

While she stood there the seated woman turned her head and the blood left Maggie's face. The plate and mug slipped from her nerveless fingers and she shook her head slowly from side to side.

This could not be happening.

The face she was looking at demonstrated how slim the line between beauty and average was; it was *her* face if her features had been perfectly symmetrical, if her lips had been less generous and her nose had been straight.

The woman stood and Maggie thought she could be looking in the mirror if she were four inches taller and half a stone lighter.

Nobody was shouting any more; they were all staring at her. She never had liked being the centre of attention, she thought, struggling to control the bubble of hysteria lodged in her throat.

The silence that had followed the shouting was unbearably loud.

'I dropped the plate.'

Her voice was the catalyst for a fresh bout of yelling. This time the woman joined in and the baby—no, *babies*—in the pram started to cry.

Feeling strangely disconnected from the drama unfolding and, for that matter, her own body, Maggie listened to the exchange of insults and accusation—a lot of accusation, and most of it aimed at Rafael, who made, it seemed to Maggie, only a token effort to defend himself.

His attention was constantly straying from those who were energetically jabbing the finger of blame at him to Maggie.

'How could you, Rafael! My daughter…you have betrayed every trust I ever had in you!'

'What gave you the right to assume…? I am not like your father…I thought we were friends…'

Maggie sucked in a breath, caught up in this strange nightmare moment but distant from it—distant from these people who were not her people.

The need for the comfort, the familiarity, of those she knew were there for her no matter what rose up inside her until she had to act on it.

'Nice to meet you, but I have to go now.'

Even though her voice had been barely more than a whisper the acoustics in the room were such that every word echoed around the room.

Silence broke out all over again.

Maggie dropped to her knees. 'I'll just…'

Rafael was at her side, taking her hand and cursing as he saw blood oozing steadily from the superficial cut.

'I could do with a dustpan, really.'

'Madre di Dios!' he breathed, lifting her into his arms.

He turned his head, murder in his eyes in response to an angry comment from the male half of the couple, before he strode up the stairs with Maggie in his arms. She didn't resist, she did not do anything—the blank look in her eyes scared him more than anything in his life!

He sat her on the bed and cleaned and dressed the wound. He pushed a glass of brandy into her hand. For a moment she looked at it blankly, then he saw something move at the back of her eyes a moment before, with calm deliberation, she tipped the contents on the floor.

'Was that who I think it is?'

'Yes, it was Your mother is married to my cousin.'

The muscles along her jaw quivered as she looked at him with dark unfriendly eyes.

'No, she isn't, because my mother,' she said in a voice that quivered and shook with emotion, 'my mother looked after me when I had chicken pox and wanted to scratch the spots—she stopped me. She read my teacher the Riot Act when I was being bullied at school. She listened to my spellings when I had a test. I only need one mother and *that* woman is nothing to me…a stranger.'

'I know it must be hard for you to understand now, but Angelina was very young and her family—'

Maggie shook her head and covered her ears. 'I don't want to know her name. I don't want to know how sad and sorry she is. I want *nothing* from her. Do you understand? *Nothing!*'

'You're pretty judgemental. Haven't you ever made a mistake?'

The question drew a bitter smile from Maggie. 'Several, but the one I'm looking at right now makes the others fade into insignificance.'

She saw him flinch as her words hit home and she didn't care. She was glad. She wanted him to hurt as much as she was, even though that was impossible.

The burst of anger had actually cleared the fog of confusion in Maggie's brain, leaving cool, clear clarity in its place. As the argument's main points sifted through her mind she looked at her bandaged hand and noticed it had stopped shaking.

'Let me get this straight—is it true what that man said?'

'Alfonso my cousin.' Who now, it seemed, hated and despised him—there was a lot of it around! The next time anyone asked his advice he was going to develop selective deafness—not that this was likely to happen any time soon;

most, if not all, of the people he cared about were not talking to him.

'Was he right? You slept with me to stop me confronting *her* and spoiling a family party. You could,' she suggested bitterly, 'have just explained it wasn't a good moment. And I wasn't…'

'You weren't?'

'I have never wanted to trace my birth mother. I even split up with Simon because he did just that and now you…' She dropped her head into her hands. Rafael had seemed so different, but actually he wasn't.

He was worse!

She pressed her fingers to her pounding temples. Rafael covered them with his own and tilted her face to his. 'I admit it started out that way…'

'And then you fell desperately in love me…yes… Save your breath, Rafael, for the next starry-eyed fool who thinks every word you utter is gospel.'

'I have never lied to you, Maggie.'

'No, but you were pretty economic with the truth and anyway you didn't need to lie, did you? Because, let's face facts, I was easy!'

Rafael swore.

Maggie flinched away from his outstretched hand. 'It was all an act, wasn't it? And in the end such a waste of your *valuable* time, because I never presented any danger. I was not a scandal waiting to happen. I was just a silly girl who believed you were as special as you seemed. And you're not, you're not special, you're…' Her voice quivered as the tears began to seep unchecked from her eyes. 'I hate you and I wish we'd never met!' She raced to the wardrobe and began to pull her possessions off the rail. 'I'm going home.'

The dark lines of colour scoring Rafael's razor-edged cheekbones deepened as he watched her. 'I did not ask you to stay with me only because of Angelina and you did not stay because you hate me.'

Maggie spun back, her dark eyes glowing with scorn. 'Like you said yourself, I'm a fast learner, and actually hating is not so hard!' Maggie drew a hand across the nape of her neck to free the hair trapped under her shirt before sweeping it back from her face and securing it behind her ears.

'Do not be dramatic.'

The terse recommendation drew a low growl of incredulity from Maggie's throat.

'You could not regret the sex any more than I do…'

Maggie's head went back as though he had struck her. She bit her trembling lip.

'You were not so open,' he charged angrily. 'You did not tell me you were a virgin.'

Maggie's jaw dropped as she shook her head in disbelief—as if what he had done could compare. 'What was I meant to do—carry a sign around my neck? Call me an idiot, but I had this crazy idea I was missing out on something marvelous, that the experience would be liberating! How was I to know that it was all hype and no substance?'

He received the information with an aggravating air of disbelief. She wondered what it would take to dent this man's ego. More than a bad review from her, clearly—though it had been noted on more than one occasion that she was a bad liar.

'That is not what you said last night.' The memory sent a surge of lust through his body that Rafael was powerless to control…

Maggie gave a sniff and fixed him with a glittering glare, channelling cynical woman of the world as she admitted, 'I'm a great actress…sigh…gasp.' She let her head fall back and moaned, *'Please…please…you're so good at this,'* before straightening up and smoothing back her hair.

'You're so marvellous blah…blah…blah… Women have

been saying what men want to hear for ever. It was a good holiday, end of story, and now I'm going home.'

He took one last look at her angry, accusing face and shrugged expressively before turning and stalking stiff-backed towards the door. He paused in the opening and turned back.

'It may suit you to play the unwilling victim now, Maggie, but we both know that you were not!'

He had vanished before she thought of a suitable response. Tears streaming down her face, she ran to the door. He was nowhere in sight but she shouted down the corridor anyway.

'My fiancé turned out to be a complete and total loser and I decided that anything had to be an improvement. I was wrong!' she threw after him, before sliding to the floor and crying her heart out.

CHAPTER THIRTEEN

IT was a month later when Rafael made a discovery: it was actually quite easy to enjoy anonymity—all a person had to do was stand in a busy casualty department on a Saturday night.

He been standing in a corner of this noisy, crowded Casualty waiting room for an hour and nobody had approached him. He got the impression that if he stayed quiet he could stand there all night and nobody would; this, however, was not his intention.

He had a plan, well, not a *plan* exactly—for the first time in his life Rafael was winging it.

Another thirty minutes passed and the novelty value of being invisible began to lose its charm for Rafael. It occurred to him as he shifted his weight from foot to foot that he might have taken the under-the-radar approach a little too far.

His jaw clenched as he continued to scan the room. He had still not caught even a glimpse of her dark head and he was losing the struggle to control his frustration.

Inaction was not his thing for a reason—it was a very unproductive method of achieving a desired end.

And his desired end remained elusive. He shifted his weight from one foot to the other and wondered how she worked in this place surrounded constantly by all this ugliness and suffering.

Rafael watched a man dressed in a security uniform approach, stop a few feet away and wait expectantly.

'Can I help you, sir?'

Rafael flashed him a look. 'I should not think so.'

The security guard, who had all the responses to belligerent or threatening behaviour—not that he wasn't extremely relieved that this tough-looking customer was displaying neither—struggled for a response to this polite but unhelpful reply.

'Have you given your details at the desk?'

'I am waiting for someone.'

'I'm afraid…Mr…?'

'Castenadas,' Rafael supplied.

He watched the inevitable flicker of recognition in the other man's eyes, and gave a philosophical shrug. Security guards tended to have a lot of time to flick through tabloids.

'Do I know you? Your face…'

Rafael was saved the necessity of responding because a smashing sound, loud enough to be heard over the general babble in the waiting area, followed by raised voices caused the man to break off.

Like everyone else Rafael turned in the direction of the sound, then he heard the cry—a cry of pain followed by the distinct sound of breaking glass.

Rafael, responding to the rush of adrenaline that flooded through his body, hit the ground running. He was through the swing doors and parting the curtain before the security guard had finished summoning help.

The scene was chaos: an overturned trolley, broken glass, instruments all over the floor and a large thug slurring a string of loud abuse at the figure crouched on the floor.

Some gut instinct had told him the cry had come from

Maggie's lips. Even so, seeing her there made him reel as though a blow had landed through his defences.

She lifted her head, saw him, gave a sob of relief and said, 'I'm fine!' despite the evidence to the contrary.

He advanced and felt his foot slip; he glanced down, saw the blood on the floor and the colour seeped out of his face. It only took him a second, a second that was long enough to realise that the gore came, not from Maggie, but from her attacker, who was standing barefoot in the broken glass, oblivious to the pain.

The realisation that the thug was going to feel it once his anaesthetic of choice wore off afforded Rafael a brief moment of savage satisfaction before he placed his hand on the man's collar and hauled him across the room.

Rafael, grimacing in distaste, moved his head back as he was hit by alcohol fumes.

He glanced over his shoulder and was relieved to see that Maggie was getting to her feet, helped by another nurse.

The drunk did not understand a word of the staccato Spanish directed at him but he did recognise the cold light in those eyes.

Rafael's lip curled in distaste as he watched the rapid transformation from aggressive to pathetic when the drunk recognised he had lost the upper hand.

The two security men relieved him of his burden and Rafael swung back to Maggie.

'What are you doing here, Rafael?' Something twisted hard in his chest when he saw her face.

He struggled to control the rage lodged in his throat. 'I am not a medic, but if you want my unqualified opinion I'd say ice might be a good idea.'

'What are you doing here, Rafael?'

Of course she knew, she had known the moment she saw

him standing in the waiting area and pointed him out to Security as a dangerous-looking character.

He was here to speak on behalf of her birth mother, Angelina Castenadas.

She could think the name now, even say it out loud, and she'd had a series of long discussions with her mum. The discussions had involved a lot of tears but she felt less threatened by the situation. It definitely helped that she now believed Mum and Dad would not feel she was being disloyal if she did have contact with her birth mother.

'Other than saving you?'

She studied his dark face hungrily, loving every strong plane and hollow. Seeing him again had made her realise that she would never be over him, she would smile, she would laugh, she would seem normal, but there would always be an empty space inside her that she *knew* he was meant to fill.

'Thank you, Rafael.'

Her brow furrowed with concern she struggled to conceal. There were lines around his mouth she had not seen before, and shadows under his eyes that made them appear haunted.

Had he lost weight?

Had he been ill?

'Who saves you when I am not around?'

'These things only happen to me when you are.' She sucked in a deep breath. 'Look, I can save you time and energy.' She lowered her eyes as her composure slipped and added huskily, 'I know why you're here.'

He stiffened, wariness sliding into his grey eyes as he met her candid gaze.

'You're here to plead my birth mother...Angelina's case.' Maggie bit her lip. 'I know I sent her letter back unopened, but since then...I've thought about it a lot and spoke with Mum and I can see that I have been unfair. I know she had reasons for giving me up and things couldn't have turned out better for me. I have a marvellous family. I would like to meet her…later…' She still struggled with the idea that it could be the positive experience her mum suggested, but she was willing to try.

The silence stretched.

'I'm sure that Angelina will be pleased that you feel this way, but that is between you and her.'

'But I thought…?'

'I came because we had something that…it was not over.' And until it was he would remain unable to function. 'I want you back.'

The breath left her body in one startled gasp. 'You want me back.'

His lifted a shoulder in an irritated shrug. 'No, I was just passing.' His eyes narrowed as he hissed, 'Why else would I be here?'

'And what I want? I suppose that is irrelevant.'

'You want me,' he charged. It was a struggle to think past the fog of sexual hunger in his brain, but this much he did know.

The predatory gleam in his eyes when he made this arrogant pronouncement sent a stab of excitement through Maggie's hopelessly receptive body.

'We can work out some sort of arrangement,' he continued casually.

'Arrangement?'

'Families need not be involved.' For the first time in his life he understood the attraction of being stranded on a desert island with no distractions.

Maggie shook her head as if waking from a daze. 'Believe me, Rafael, you're not the sort of man I'd take home to meet my parents.' What did you expect, Maggie? she asked herself bitterly. That he came here because he's interested in you anywhere outside the bedroom?

He studied her flushed, angry face with a baffled expression. 'Why are you behaving as though I have insulted you?'

She pressed a finger to her chin and pretended to consider the question. 'Could it have something to do with the fact that you think all you have to do is snap your fingers and I'll provide sex on tap?'

His face darkened with anger at her sarcasm. 'You would have sex on tap also.'

The mortified colour flew to her cheeks at the taunt. 'You're not the only man in the world or, for that matter, my life,' she lied.

For a moment Rafael could not breathe past the swell of molten hot anger in his chest.

'I'm curious,' she continued, oblivious to his titanic struggle for control. 'Are we talking about just while you are in town, days or weeks...hours? Or are you asking me to move in and be your full-time mistress?'

'You wish to formalise the arrangement?' His shoulders lifted. 'Fine...yes!'

The mocking smile slid from her lips. 'You're not serious!'

'I would not be here unless I was serious.' Or insane, he thought, dragging a hand through his dark hair. 'You walked away from me. No woman has ever done that.'

'So this is about pride.' Maggie was furious with herself for imagining even for one brief second that it might be more. 'We're not finished until *you* say so...'

He regarded her with an expression of intense irritation. 'Why do you always twist what I say? I have come here—'

Her lips twisted. 'I'm flattered.'

'You should be. I've never chased after a woman in my life.'

Maggie's eyes swept upwards and connected with his brooding molten stare; her breath caught. 'You're chasing me?'

His fascinating mouth curved upwards. 'I've caught you.'

A shiver slid down her spine and she swayed towards him as though drawn by an invisible thread.

'Mags…?'

A nurse popped her head around the curtain that someone had pulled across and Rafael stepped back, the muscle in his lean cheek clenching as he swore under his breath.

'Mark will give your eye the once-over shortly.' The girl slid a curious and appreciative glance toward Rafael. 'He's just seeing to our friend. The guy's feet are in a mess—he was walking on glass.'

'No problem, I'm fine. I'll be out in a minute.'

'Can I get your friend anything…coffee, tea…?'

Maggie, who heard the unspoken addition of *me,* glared and heard Rafael respond with an abrupt, 'No.'

Rafael, who had listened to the brief interchange with growing disbelief, waited until the other woman had left before he spoke. 'That man—he is being attended to before you.'

'Well, it is a matter of priorities.'

Indeed it was, and the ones he was witnessing were to his mind, sadly skewed.

'You are planning on continuing to work?'

She nodded. 'It's a really busy evening and we're short staffed…'

Rafael unable to contain his outrage a moment longer held up his hand. 'Listen to me—you are *not* going back to work.'

'Really, Rafael, you don't understand—'

'No, you don't understand—this is not a debate.'

'You can't walk in here and order me about. I'm not your live-in girlfriend yet…not yet, I mean…' She closed her eyes and thought, What do I mean? Her head felt as though someone were inside her skull trying to hammer his way out. 'All right, I'll go home once I've been checked.'

Rafael's feelings were not soothed long. When the doctor did put in an appearance he looked as though he had not begun shaving and his manner towards Maggie was far too familiar.

The doctor pronounced her fine, though he suggested she might like to wear dark glasses for a few days because she was going to have quite a shiner.

He also said there was no way she should go back to work. This time Maggie did not argue; the man with the hammer in her skull had been joined by friends. Maggie looked up as Rafael stepped back into the room.

'You're still here?'

Rafael's dark brows shot up. 'You expected me not to be? We have things to discuss.'

Maggie's lashes fell. 'Not tonight…'

'Certainly tonight,' he retorted, his attitude displaying no room for manoeuvre.

'Fine. I can save you some time, Rafael. I can't be…with you.'

A muscle clenched in his cheek. 'Why?'

'Because I can't be with a man who can't promise me an exclusive relationship that lasts more than a few weeks.' With a highly sexed man like Rafael, she thought dourly, there would always be someone waiting to take her place.

A nerve clenched in his lean cheek and he remained silent as he pushed open the swing doors for her to pass through before him.

'And if I was prepared to do that?'

Eyes round in amazement, she swung back just as a blinding light flashed in her face. Beside her Rafael swore, raised his arm to shield her, moving to stand between her and the paparazzo.

'Just keep walking.'

A good plan in theory, but she stumbled and Rafael swept

her up into his arms and across to the waiting car, all the time being snapped.

Maggie gave a sigh of relief as the car pulled away.

Rafael flashed her a quick sideways look. 'We should be at my place in about half an hour, traffic willing.'

'I want to go to *my* place and it will take five minutes.'

It actually took less than the five minutes she predicted and Rafael hadn't said another word after his abrupt, 'Fine!' when he turned the ignition.

It didn't occur to Maggie to ask how he knew where she lived as she responded to his urging to hurry because the paparazzo would not be far behind.

The flat door closed and the tension slid from Maggie's shoulders and she flopped down onto the sofa. 'God that awful man.'

'There will be more awful men when you move in with me,' Rafael felt obliged to warn her as he pulled down his sleeve to cover the nick on his wrist that was still seeping blood.

'If I move in…' Maggie stopped, her eyes drawn by his actions to the stain on the cuff of his shirt. 'You're bleeding!' she accused, leaping to her feet.

Rafael gave an impatient shrug. 'It's nothing—a piece of glass, I think…'

'Let me see? You should have let someone look at it.'

Rafael backed away. 'It's nothing.'

'It should be cleaned.'

He stifled his impatience and gave a sigh. 'Fine, where's your bathroom? I'll wash it if that will make you happy.' Nothing but feeling her body beneath him would make him happy.

Maggie directed him and sat listening to the sound of running water.

It was a few moments later he emerged, his face and hair both dripping wet; he barely seemed to register the fact.

Dazed was the only word she could think of to describe his expression.

Oh, God, maybe he had a thing about blood?

She shot to her feet. 'Sit down, you look…'

Acting as if he hadn't heard her, he walked straight past her and headed for the door. 'Rafael!' she called after him, seriously spooked by his strange behaviour. 'Where are you going?'

He swung back and she saw the dazed look in his eyes had been replaced by a grim but purposeful gleam. 'I will make things right. Stay indoors until I get back.'

And with that he was gone.

CHAPTER FOURTEEN

MAGGIE covered her ears as the phone began to ring again. She clenched her teeth, willing it to stop. When it did she let out a long sibilant sigh of relief and felt like an utter coward as she carried on searching for her other shoe.

Where had she put the damned thing?

'Calm down and think, Maggie,' she muttered, recalling that she had been sitting in her armchair when she began to cry.

She had sat puzzling over Rafael's enigmatic words while she had waited and waited some more, but he hadn't come back. At some point in the early hours it occurred to her that she could spend the next few months doing just that—waiting.

What sort of man, she asked herself suggested living together and walked out before they had discussed it? A man who had cold feet? It was then she realised that it was never going to work—they had no sort of future together.

She resumed her search, angrily dashing tears from her cheeks, but it was unsuccessful and the respite before the phone started ringing again was brief.

She knew who it was without checking the caller ID again. He had called the first time an hour earlier and without thinking she had picked it up; the sound of his deep voice the other end had caused her to drop the receiver.

It had been ringing every few seconds since and she had been ignoring it. Maybe not ignoring—ignoring suggested she was tuning out the sound and carrying on with what she was doing, which was of course thinking about Rafael. When wasn't she thinking about Rafael?

She was just not answering because she was a pathetic coward. While she didn't answer she could pretend he had a perfectly good explanation for running out of there last night.

The only solution—why hadn't she thought of it earlier?— she decided, was to get out of the flat with or without her shoes. Of course, she *could* answer, but that would mean hearing his voice and how badly she wanted to—simple *want* didn't really describe the intense, deep, gut-wrenching longing—was so utterly terrifying that she just couldn't do it.

It could be the first step on the slippery slope: this time answering the phone, the next time ringing his number just so she could hear his voice!

Last night he had literally run from her flat as though he couldn't bear to be in her company—if ever there was a case of actions speaking louder than words, that was it!

Ditching her shoe search, she ran to the door where she'd left her trainers—why had she fixated on the black heels anyhow?—and began to lace them up with shaky fingers.

It was far too easy, she reflected to get into the mindset of thinking she had no control.

'I do have control. I won't love him.'

She angrily wiped a tear from her cheek and almost immediately realised she couldn't *not* love him.

Halfway down the stairs, her thoughts in utter turmoil, she realised she had not got her car keys. She retraced her steps and discovered she had left her door wide open.

I'm losing it, she thought.

Rafael's dark features flashed into her head and she sighed, thinking, You lost it the moment Rafael-Luis Castenadas smiled at you and since then you've been in denial big time.

Denial didn't seem so bad when she considered the alternatives.

She was reaching into her bag for a tissue when she walked straight into the blinding volley of flashes.

Confused she blinked and lifted a hand to shield her eyes as the waiting press pack advanced.

And this time they were here in force.

They were all talking at once, several were waving newspapers in her face, and all she could think as she stood there was how odd that they knew her name.

'Miss Ward, are you going to press charges?'

'Maggie, has this ever happened before? Has he hit you before?'

'Miss Ward, is it true that Rafael Castenadas attacked you while you were trying to save the life of a—'

The questions hit her like missiles as the cameras kept flashing. Maggie shrank back in horror, her feet nailed to the spot.

'Maggie, if you give us an exclusive we can get you out of here.'

Maggie focused on the man that had come close, his face right in hers. She could smell his aftershave and she stopped being scared and started being angry—very angry.

He took another step towards her, his face arranged in a sympathetic smile, and suddenly the feeling returned to her paralysed limbs.

He extended his hand towards her and she lifted her chin and said, 'I don't think so. Now move out of my way.'

He looked taken aback by the low note of cold authority in her clear voice, but he didn't budge. None of them did; it was a scrum.

Like pack animals scenting blood—hers, which was not a nice thought—they continued to yell and jostle, physically blocking her exit and trapping her.

Head down, struggling to emulate the air of cold indifference with which Rafael treated the press intrusion, and failing miserably, Maggie tried to push her way through the screaming mass.

Of course, they would not have bumped and shoved him, not even the keenest paparazzo would have made that mistake.

'Is it true the police want to question Rafael?'

Maggie's head came up; the red dots dancing before her eyes formed a red mist and, eyes blazing, she rounded on the man who had spoken.

'What did you say?'

'Are the police questioning Rafe, Maggie?'

Wrapping herself in a cloak of icy dignity, Maggie lifted her chin and fixed the man with a direct unblinking regard. 'The police are *not* interested in questioning *Mr Castenadas,* but they will be interested in questioning you if you don't take your hand off my arm.'

She held his eyes until his hand fell away, then she nodded and said quietly, 'Thank you.'

She managed to move another couple of feet forward before the pack closed in around her once more.

'Do you think you're setting a bad example to other abused women by not bringing charges?'

Maggie could almost hear the sound of control snapping. She threw up her hands as anger coursed through her veins.

'That's it!' she cried, swinging back to face the general direction the question had come from. 'How dare you take the moral high ground and preach to me?' As if they were interested in anything but a headline.

In this situation Rafael would have acted as if they didn't exist and he would never have tried to defend himself.

But she wasn't Rafael and she couldn't stand by and let them say these things about him while he wasn't even there to defend himself—she just couldn't!

'I don't know how you lot get away with saying things like this about a man who…' She stopped, her throat closing over with emotion as she added furiously, 'God, you're not fit to breathe the same air as him. For the record, my black eye is courtesy of a patient who got nasty in Casualty, but a drunk hitting a nurse isn't much of a story, is it? It's the stuff that happens every day.' She paused and let her contemptuous gaze move over the now silent crowd.

'You don't send out the cameras for that, do you? Oh, no, that's not *sexy* news,' she spat scornfully. 'You'd prefer to make up lies about a man whose only crime is not crossing to the other side of the street when someone needs help, I wonder how many of you can say the same?'

The silence grew and, shaking with emotion, Maggie looked directly into the camera lens pointed at her face. 'I don't know how you're going to sell this as being in the public interest. Rafael's only crime is being successful and good to look at.'

She paused to catch her breath and thought, Maybe, just maybe I have got through to them—when one small voice broke the silence.

'So what's it feel like to be the girlfriend of a billionaire, Maggie?'

The question signalled the return of hostilities after the brief lull. The questions came thick, fast and frequently offensive. Maggie stood, her fists clenched, unable to defend herself from the onslaught. Her emotional outburst had utterly exhausted her emotional defences.

She wanted to run, but she couldn't; they were pressing in on her from all sides.

She stiffened as she felt arms slide around her waist and instinctively began to hit out wildly.

Her flailing elbow made contact and Maggie felt a spurt of savage satisfaction when she heard a grunt of pain.

'I come in peace.'

At the familiar voice Maggie stilled. She had elbowed Rafael. She stifled a totally inappropriate desire to giggle—probably hysteria—and said his name.

She said it again because it sounded good, then added, 'Some people say better late than never, but I don't.'

'That is something we will speak of soon. For now just relax—we'll be out of here in one minute. Trust me.'

Maggie did utterly, which was totally crazy because he didn't represent safety and he had gone all weird and left her high and dry last night. Rafael represented rampant sexuality, dangerous excitement and misery because he couldn't love her.

Even while she acknowledged this she leaned back with a sigh of relief into the hard solidity of his lean male body feeling his strength seep into her—a physiological impossibility, but true nonetheless.

On one level she recognised that her reliance on him was foolish. Hadn't she always solved her own problems? She was no wilting flower. Yet here she was, leaning, and not just physically, on Rafael... It was actually just good to be able to let go and know that someone else would pick up the pieces...was that wrong?

The thoughts passed through her head in a matter of seconds, though time had little meaning to Maggie as around them the flashes became one continuous blast of light and the barrage of questions and requests to look at the camera became a hysterical babble.

Rafael, partially shielded from the press pack by the physical presence of the two broad-shouldered figures, with a combination of expertise and their sheer bulk, were shielding the couple, turned Maggie around to face him and winced.

The sight of her poor face sent a blast of outrage through him, followed swiftly by an equally powerful stab of protective tenderness.

He had spent his entire adult life keeping, not just women, but his emotions at arm's length and succeeding—until Maggie came along.

His emotional detachment had been crumbling from the moment he had laid eyes on her, he'd just been too blind to see it, but last night when those baby clothes had spilled out of the boxes in her bathroom and he had realised she was carrying his baby it had disintegrated and his vision had cleared!

Marriage, love, children—they were all things he had never wanted or needed. Ironically the very things he had actively avoided were now the things Rafael wanted more than anything.

He wanted Maggie, but after the way he had behaved he knew he had a lot of ground to make up. But he had made a start, and he would do whatever it took to convince her that he would be a good husband and father.

'You do know you've turned my life upside down, don't you, Maggie Ward?' He touched her uninjured cheek and tilted her head a little to one side to examine the bruises.

If he had that loser from yesterday here now… His hands tightened into fists and he told himself that violence never solved anything. On the other hand it would make him feel a lot better.

Pushing away the thoughts of retribution, he curled his fingers gently around her chin and turned her face to examine the damage that appeared to be limited to the right side.

Maggie withstood his silent scrutiny with difficulty. Where was a paper bag when a girl needed it?

'The bruising has come out today.' Rafael, without her experience of similar injuries, probably found the sight more shocking than she had; he might not realise it was actually very superficial.

Maggie knew that tomorrow when the swelling began to subside she would be able to disguise most of the damage with make-up, but it had been a lost cause today.

Rafael swore through clenched teeth and, without taking his eyes from her face, lifted a hand to signal to the two men who had exited the car that had pulled up on the kerb behind the chauffeur-driven limo he and the first security contingent had arrived in.

Maggie, totally unaware of them moving into place beside the limo, unconscious of anything but Rafael, shook her head when he observed in a strained, thickened voice, 'It must be very painful.'

'Actually it—'

He laid a finger against her lips. 'If you are about to say, "It looks worse than it is," do not.'

How did he know?

'And if you go into brave little trouper mode I will not be responsible for my actions.'

Maggie did not get the opportunity to ask him if he preferred she have hysterics as at that moment one of the big minders said something in Spanish. Rafael listened and nodded. Maggie, who up until that point had not even realised Rafael was not alone, watched as the man, complete with dark suit and mirrored shades, spoke into a mouthpiece, then said something in rapid Spanish to Rafael, who nodded in agreement.

'You brought reinforcements?'

Rafael, recalling the moment he had drawn up and seen her in the middle of the media feeding frenzy, swallowed a retort.

If it had not been for the intervention of Luis, he might have waded in metaphorical guns blazing and made a bad situation worse. The way he was feeling now made him think it might have been worth it.

Dios, at that moment he hated diplomacy; he loathed tactics. Frustration at being forced to stifle his natural impulses left the adrenaline with no place to go but notching up the tension in his body to a painful level.

'This is my Head of Security, Luis,' he said, introducing the man at his shoulder to Maggie.

The man with the mirrored shades inclined his shaved head and might have smiled, it was hard to tell, but Maggie smiled back just in case. He struck her as the sort of man you didn't want to offend.

'If I'd known you would be *stupid* enough to walk into this I would have fetched a small army.'

Maggie's attention swung back to Rafael, eyes widened indignantly as she launched into a robust defence of her actions. 'How was I to know that they'd—?'

'Save it!' he snapped, cutting her off with an impatient motion of his dark head.

Her chin went up in response to the autocratic decree. 'But I—'

'Just do what I say and do not argue, also do not speak.'

Maggie nodded meekly, her eyes dropping as she recalled her diatribe.

The entire face-the-press-and-yell-at-them thing was all a bit of a blur. But she had yelled, yes, there had definitely been volume—this she knew even though the content of her rant remained frustratingly elusive.

Around them there was noise and frenetic activity, but everything about Rafael, from his carved features to his steady regard, was still. But nobody would mistake that stillness for tranquillity.

Fascinated by the resolution she saw etched into every

stunning angle of his lean face, Maggie stared. Resolution, not to be confused with coolness, and the light gleaming in his eyes had a combustible quality that was echoed in his body language.

His black leather jacket open to reveal a blue shirt that deepened the intense startling colour of his eyes, he reminded Maggie of a dark avenging angel.

A shiver trickled down her spine and things shifted and clenched low and deep inside her as she stared, her eyes drawn to the muscle clenching and unclenching along his shadowed jaw.

She was frightened by the dangerous idea that surfaced in her brain: to touch him, run her fingers over his hair-roughened cheek. Once planted, the impulse was almost impossible to resist. She pressed her clenched hands to her chest, and silently mouthed, No!

Either he could read lips or she had not been so silent because Rafael bent forward and said, 'There is no need to be frightened of them.'

Just of you she thought. 'Easy for you to say—you're the sort of person who gets a kick from chasing hurricanes.'

'A hurricane,' he observed bitterly, 'is child's play compared to you!'

It was always good to have the man you loved inform you that you were a nightmare. Maggie opened her mouth to deliver a suitably ironic response and was horrified to feel her eyes fill.

Rafael watched her luminous eyes fill and felt a pain that was roughly the equivalent of having a dagger plunged into his chest.

He snarled something very un-angelic and wrapped an arm supportively around her waist. She saw the muscles in his brown throat work as he framed her face with his free hand, angling it up to him.

His eyes swept her pale features again, a spasm twisting his lips into a pained grimace as he made himself look again at the extent of the damage to her cheek and eye.

Maggie went instinctively to lift a protective hand to her face, but found she couldn't. Her hand was trapped between their bodies and the fingers of her free hand had somehow become interlaced with Rafael's.

Maggie stared at the brown fingers wrapped around her own wondering when that happened as Rafael swore soft and savage under his breath as one of his minders spoke.

The muscles along his jaw tightened as he turned his attention back to Maggie. This madness was his life, not hers—what had he got her into?

'This,' he said, self-condemnation putting a harsh uneven note into his deep voice as he flicked a harsh glare at the media pack. 'It should not have happened.' He touched the bruised, discoloured skin tenderly with the pad of his thumb and swore again, turning his head as he closed his eyes and clamped his jaw.

Maggie's eyelashes came down in a protective sweep, a turbulent cocktail of emotions lodged tight like a weight in her chest as she struggled to hold back the hot tears that stung her eyelids.

She was vaguely conscious of a flurry of movement as one of the minders confiscated the camera someone had pushed under Rafael's nose. He acted as though nothing had happened.

Maggie wondered enviously how he managed that.

And how did he put up with this sort of invasion on a daily basis? How did he tune out the press who dogged his footsteps?

Presumably this was why he had adopted a strict policy of 'say nothing, not even yes or no' and, though the details still remained a bit of a blur she was pretty sure she had said more than that and it would probably be edited to suit whatever angle they were pursuing.

She took a deep breath. Better to come clean now before she lost her nerve.

'I didn't keep my mouth shut. I said...stuff.'

The guilty admission brought his eyes to the mouth in question. Lust slammed through his body. That was predictable, if painful, but the protective instincts that accompanied it were so alien to him still, so strong, that his normal restraint snapped.

Didn't consider the audience or their cameras, but the need that drove him as he framed her face in his hands.

Didn't consider them as he bent his head.

Didn't consider them as he fitted his mouth to hers and with a groan of male need slid his tongue deep into the soft heat of her mouth.

The paparazzi, unable to believe their luck at the cool, controlled Rafael Castenadas' public display, went crazy as they snapped the kissing couple.

Rafael lifted his head.

Dazed and clinging to Rafael's jacket Maggie was vaguely aware of Rafael's extended arm protecting her and bodies, encouraged by their escorts, parting to let them through to the waiting car.

The door, held open and flanked by another two tough-looking suited figures who were both talking into headpieces, was closed with a decisive sound after Rafael slid into the back seat beside her.

Rafael spoke to the driver and leaned back in his seat as the car moved off and the smoked-glass partition between them slid into place.

Maggie willed herself not to lower her gaze, while for the first time she started asking herself why he was here.

His glance skimmed her profile. 'I am sorry that you had

to go through that,' he said, sounding angry, which, considering he was the one that had done the kissing, struck Maggie as pretty unreasonable.

'I told you to stay in and I did try and warn you,' he added.

'Did you?'

Maggie could not recall any warning.

Just the memory of his mouth, she mused her glance drawn irresistibly to that strongly sculpted sensual curve. And his probing tongue sliding—that was very clear. She huffed a shaky breath and, sliding her fingers into her heavy hair, pushed it from her face. The memory was not so easy to remove; it lingered like the heat lying low in her pelvis.

'I've been ringing all morning.'

'Ringing?' she echoed blankly.

'You were not picking up.'

'I was busy,' she lied.

His public display had been totally out of character, so possibly she was irresistible?

If that were true he would hardly have walked away last night.

Or—a less flattering though possibly more likely explanation—it had been a dramatic way of telling the circus that dogged his footsteps that they did not make any impact on his life—Rafael's way of thumbing his nose at them.

He clenched his teeth in frustration and pushed his head back deep into the soft upholstery as he closed his eyes. 'You were not busy, you were simply punishing me because I walked out last night.' His eyes opened. 'There was a reason.'

Maggie shook her head and betrayed no interest in hearing it.

What was the point? Nothing, with the exception of hearing him say he loved her, would make anything better—and that was not going to happen.

He studied the obstinate angle of her averted chin and said softly, 'Look at me, Maggie.'

Maggie ignored the instruction and carried on staring at the smoked-glass window.

She listened to him curse fluently, then turned her head. 'I want to go home.'

'We are.'

She looked at him, a question in her narrowed eyes.

'Going home, to my London house. We can be private there.'

'I don't want to be private,' she retorted, thinking that it was a pity he hadn't been so keen on privacy before he gave the photo opportunity of a decade to the paparazzi.

'Why did you agree?'

She was thrown by the question and her startled gaze flew to his face, her first mistake—his compelling metallic stare shredded her thin veneer of composure.

She cleared her throat and tugged fretfully at the neck of her top. 'Agree to what?'

'To meeting Angelica—why did you agree?'

'Why the third degree? I thought that's what you wanted.'

'And you always do what I want?' He loosed a dry laugh and reminded her, 'Before you gave the very strong impression that your mind was made up, you were totally inflexible on the subject, unwavering…'

Maggie's eyes fell from the disturbing speculation in his silver gaze.

'I wasn't.'

'You were dead set against it.'

Maggie focused at some point over his shoulder God if only it were that easy to ignore him! She was painfully conscious of him.

'Things change,' she countered.

'And what changed with you?'

Maggie lifted her head in response to the pressure of his fingers under her chin. She shook her head mutely.

'Susan thinks you might be pregnant.'

CHAPTER FIFTEEN

MAGGIE'S eyes went wide with shock. For the space of several heartbeats her breathing was suspended. The colour seeped from her already pale cheeks before she took a deep gulping breath.

If she had not been sitting her legs would have failed her.

That statement did not work on more levels than she could count.

'Susan…Mum…?'

He confirmed her incredulous query with a calm nod of his head. 'An incredible woman,' he said. "Like her daughter."

Talking long into the night with her parents had helped him understand what had made Maggie the woman she was today—too mature for her years in many ways, yet untouched…*until he came along.*

He clenched his teeth against the self-condemnatory stab of self-loathing that sliced into him like a dull blade when he considered the impact his selfish actions had had on the one person in the world he wanted to protect.

Madre di Dios, he seemed to have inherited an uncanny ability to mess up when it came to the people he loved…

He could only imagine how Maggie must be feeling.

She'd spent all her life weighed down by responsibilities. This was her time, her time to finally put her needs and desires above those of others, her time to be carefree, and if her mother's suspicions were correct he was responsible for clipping her wings before she had spread them.

Maggie had no control over the rush of pleasure she experienced at the compliment. Her throat clogged with emotion she struggled not to show, it was one of the nicest things that anyone had ever said to her.

'You do know that I'm not her real daughter?' She stopped—of course he did.

With an expressive sweep of his hand Rafael brushed aside the comment as irrelevant. 'She has passed on her qualities to you, strength, compassion, and, I suspect,' he added, flashing a grin that sent her sensitive stomach into a lurching dive, 'bloody-minded stubbornness.'

Maggie stared at him in a daze. 'You *really* spoke to her? *When* did you speak to her? She thinks I'm…' A slow flush worked its way up her neck until her face was burning.

Rafael's eyes didn't leave her face. 'And is she right, Maggie?' he asked quietly.

Maggie struggled to tear her eyes from the nerve pulsing like a metronome beside his mouth, and she was not fooled by his conversational tone. Even though his hand had fallen away, she could feel the waves of tension rolling off his lean body.

'How can you have spoken to my mum?' It seemed better to deal with one extraordinary comment at a time. 'You don't even know her phone number.'

The moment the words left her lips she knew how stupid they were. It was hardly beyond his capabilities to pick up a telephone book or have a flunky do it for him.

Delegated or not, why would he want to?

'I did not phone your mother—'

'I didn't think so—'

'I called on her. The term "jaw dropped" has just taken on

an entirely new meaning,' he observed, placing a helpful finger under her chin. Maggie's mouth closed with an audible click as she continued to stare at him.

He stared back, allowing himself the luxury of examining the delicate features turned to him, committing each soft curve and delicate hollow to memory. As emotions that he had finally stopped fighting welled up he tried to put them in words, but for once in his life the words wouldn't come.

Instead he mumbled huskily, 'A better look for you I feel.'

Maggie shivered as he trailed a finger over the curve of her cheek.

He thinks you're pregnant.

Her brows twitched together in a dark line of distrust as she wrinkled her nose. 'How do you mean "called on her"?' she quizzed suspiciously.

'What part of "called on her" do you not follow? You wish for me to describe my actions step by step?'

He gave every appearance of being amused, relaxed even but, noting the more defined foreign inflection in his voice—something she had previously noticed occurred at moments of heightened emotion—Maggie wondered if he might not actually be so stress free as he appeared.

Of course he's not stress free, dunce, she told herself scornfully. He's trying to figure out if you're about to lumber him with a baby he definitely doesn't want. Wow, was he going to be happy when she set him straight—he might also feel less inclined to tell her she was beautiful.

Ignoring the stab of pain administered by this timely reality check, she snapped, 'Do what you like.' Spoiling the delivery by allowing a quiver of emotion to ruin her snarl.

She saw him register the quiver, felt him tense for a moment, and thought he was about to reach for her. When he didn't the relief—or was it the anticlimax?—was intense.

'I knocked on the door, and she let me in, or to be precise

your brother let me in…Sam, I think? They are both very alike.'

This comment dragged her wandering thoughts back from the confused dark place they had fled. Wide eyes flew to his face.

'Sam has the broken nose.' This conversation had gone past surreal.

'Then it was Sam,' Rafael confirmed. 'Susan was late back from her physiotherapy appointment.'

Maggie blinked at the casual familiarity of the comment. 'Will you stop talking as if you know my family?' she pleaded, pushing both hands into her dark hair.

'*Know* might be overstating it,' he admitted. 'But I felt we got on well.'

'You really went to my house?' She eyed him with suspicion, and wondered if this was his idea of a joke.

'I did, last night.'

'You went to my house.' She shook her head as she tried to imagine Rafael in his immaculate designer suit and handmade leather shoes in her parents' chintzy living room, complete with its out-of-tune piano and large shaggy dog, and failed.

Talk about worlds colliding!

He crossed one ankle over the other and raised his brows. 'Why do you find this fact so extraordinary?'

'Why?' She laughed. 'Because you're—' her gesture took in his elegant person from sleek dark head to gleaming handmade shoes '—*you* and my family are…' She stopped. 'What were you doing there anyway?'

'I wanted to explain the situation to your parents before they woke up this morning and saw this.'

Maggie's eyes shifted to the paper he rustled. She was turning back to him when she registered the photo splashed across the front page and felt the pain behind her eyes kick up several uncomfortable notches.

She closed her eyes and breathed deeply, her freckles standing out against the marble pallor of her skin. Rafael, a breath trapped in his throat, frustration lodged like a fist in his chest, felt every protective instinct he possessed screaming for him to make her feel better, but how?

He was reaching out when she opened her eyes.

'Fame at last,' she said faintly. 'Some people try all their lives to make the front cover.' It was a struggle to treat the situation like a joke when she thought of all the people she knew who would be looking at it. 'Not very flattering,' she finished hoarsely.

Rafael, his eyes welded to her face, watched her lips quiver and cursed. The violence of the mumbled epithet brought her eyes to his face.

'It could have been worse.'

Maggie stared at the brown fingers covering hers and gulped, resisting a mad impulse to throw herself into his arms. As if that were going to solve anything…though it would feel nice while it lasted.

Maggie didn't believe him but appreciated the white lie.

'I didn't think…' she admitted with a shamefaced grimace as she thought of her parents picking the newspaper up off the mat and seeing that.

He took the newspaper away and slung it over his shoulder. 'You have other things on your mind.' Like carrying my baby. 'I have been there before, though not with anyone like you.'

The concession made her stiffen. He did not need to labour the point that he was not normally photographed with a woman who looked as seductive as a scarecrow.

'I'm so sorry if it's injured your reputation to be seen with a woman who is fully dressed and not drop-dead gorgeous!'

Dark head tilted to one side, he regarded her with an air of frustrated incredulity. 'You have a positive genius for mis-interpreting everything I say. The women I have been photo-graphed with previously have been with me because they want to be photographed, not because of my charming per-sonality. They want their five minutes of fame.'

'Well, don't flatter yourself. I wasn't with you because of your charming personality. You're not charming, you're a...a...' She stopped and thought, The man I love, before adding with a husky note of enquiry, 'Mum and Dad...'

'They know that you are all right. I wanted them to stay with friends but they preferred to sit it out.'

'You mean the press are there too?' Maggie asked, startled. That had not even occurred to her.

'A few when I left this morning.'

Maggie groaned.

'Look on the bright side—your brothers are anticipating an upsurge in female interest in the near future.'

The comment drew a reluctant laugh from Maggie. She could almost hear the boys. 'You really were there,' she said wonderingly.

'I like your family, Magdalena.'

'Me too. I suppose I should thank you for making the effort...?' Her eyelashes came down in a protective sweep. 'So what did you say to them?'

'We had quite a long talk...'

She clenched her teeth in frustration at the evasion. 'About?'

'You, mostly.'

Maggie found this cryptic utterance deeply disturbing. 'Sure because I'm such a fascinating subject.'

'I wouldn't call you a subject.'

'No, just a total pain in the neck, probably.'

She tensed when Rafael leaned across without warning and fastened the clasp on her seat belt. 'A legal requirement.'

Rigid, Maggie sat as still as a statue while he performed his task, staring through the mesh of her lashes at the top of his dark head, her nostrils flaring in response to the evocative scent of his clean washed hair. In her head she could see herself pushing her fingers deep into the luxuriant mass.

She released a small sigh of relief when he straightened up. It was becoming increasingly difficult to maintain a semblance of sanity when she became a mass of craving hormones every time he so much as glanced her way.

As he leaned back in his seat Rafael's eyes brushed her flushed face. Maggie, her palms damp with the effort of maintaining eye contact, was too caught up in her own struggle to notice the dark bands of colour etched across the angles of his razor-edged cheekbones.

'You inspire strong feelings in everyone who meets you.'

This cryptic response drew a frown from Maggie. Thanks for nothing, she thought. 'How tactful.'

'Tact is not something I'm known for.

'You didn't tell me that you were your mother's carer when you were younger.'

Maggie's air of studied nonchalant defiance fell away at this, she felt a surge of anger.

'I was not her carer. We all mucked in. Mum was always very independent.'

'That's not what she said.'

'I wouldn't know—I wasn't there. You were talking about me behind my back.'

'Did you never resent that you didn't have a normal childhood?'

His curiosity made Maggie see red. She drew herself up poker-straight, ignoring the pain from the belt digging into her bruised shoulder as anger burned away the last shreds of her restraint.

'Of course I never resented Mum or anything else—I had

a great childhood. Don't you *dare* feel sorry for me!' she growled. '*I'm* not the one with the hang-ups and emotional scars, I can express my feelings. I don't have to reduce everything to the lowest common denominator—' She stopped, appalled by what she had said. 'I'm sorry, I shouldn't have said that…' Maggie cast a stricken look at his face before her eyes fell. 'My parents would never discuss me with a total stranger.'

'You had sex with a total stranger.' He watched her flinch and shook his head, regret etched in the drawn lines of his strong features. 'Now we have both said things we should not have. I'm not a total stranger, Maggie.'

The emotion she heard in the husky addition brought her head up, but it was not anger she saw stamped on his dark features; it was a raw need that made her stomach muscles contract and flip.

Her eyelids, suddenly heavy, half closed as she registered the sensual glow in his eyes. She struggled to retain control; she felt an erotic shiver trickle down her spine.

Control…? She swallowed and ran her tongue over her dry lips. Who was she kidding?

She definitely had more control over the direction her glance drifted than she did the dramatic dilation of her pupils. As her eyes moved slowly across the sensual curve of his incredible mouth she thought about his lips on hers, his tongue sliding into her mouth.

'*Maggie.*'

The sound of her name brought her eyes back to his, the tension climbed as she read the silent message in his hot hooded stare. A tiny gasp left her lips as desire tightened like a fist low in her belly.

The fog of sexual tension in the confined space grew denser, almost tangible and totally unbearable, she felt torn apart as conflicting desires and fears battled inside her skull.

She lifted a hand to her heaving chest as she struggled to draw enough air into her lungs.

She could almost see the breaking point she was about to collide with when a sudden thump on the car broke the spell. She jumped instinctively towards Rafael.

'Relax.'

Maggie was too tense to register the rough-edged strain in his thickened voice as he soothed her.

'What?' she asked as the car slowed and she heard several more thuds.

Then Rafael was drawing her towards him. 'It's just the reporters camped outside my place. This will only take a minute and we'll be inside.'

Maggie silently accepted the support of the arm he placed across the back of the seat; she tried to tune out the sound of muffled yells outside and the further thuds on the paintwork of the limo as she responded to the pressure of the fingers on her shoulder and shuffled her bottom across the space separating them.

She allowed her head to rest on his shoulder closing her eyes as his arm tightened around her. It was such a relief to stop fighting for a minute and give her natural instincts free rein. She felt his fingers light on skin as he brushed the hair from her brow, and she sighed, allowing herself to enjoy the intimacy that she craved.

'We're here.'

Maggie lifted her head. She hadn't even been aware of the car stopping, but the driver was standing holding the door open. She saw that they were in what appeared to be an underground parking area.

Maggie in the grip of emotions too strong and unfamiliar for her to put a name to, felt a strong reluctance to move and break the intimacy of the moment. Misinterpreting her hesitation, Rafael placed an encouraging hand between her shoulder blades.

Once they left the limo he immediately went to speak to the man he had introduced as Luis, who had climbed out of the second limo that had been travelling close on their tail the whole way. Of the car that had preceded them there was no sign.

Trying to orientate herself, Maggie stood and watched the two men speak. The shaven head of the shorter man turned in Maggie's direction several times and she felt increasingly uncomfortable. What, she wondered, were they saying about her?

Behind the respectful attitude, what were Rafael's staff saying about her?

Was she just getting paranoid?

She watched as the other man got into the car, which reversed at speed towards large electrically controlled doors that opened, letting in a blast of noise before silently closing behind it.

'Where are we?' she asked as Rafael joined her.

'This is my London home.'

'Is this where you wanted me to come yesterday?' she asked. 'Go on,' she added. 'Say it—you're right…'

Rafael's dark brows lifted at her accusing tone but the corners of his wide mouth lifted as he dragged a hand across the dark shadow on his normally clean-shaven jaw and he nodded agreement. 'Generally, but could you narrow it a little? What particular *rightness* are we discussing at the moment?'

'If I'd let you bring me here last night none of that craziness would have happened.' Maggie shrugged in the direction of the big electric doors that shielded them from prying eyes.

She turned her head and found his eyes were welded to her face, a raw, hungry expression that made her hopelessly susceptible heart thud loud against her ribs glowing in the grey depths.

'Don't look at me like that.'

The husky plea made him blink and shake his head as if dispelling a mental image.

'The women I know dress to impress,' he said, still seeing the jewelled collar around her neck.

The collar he had found himself buying two days ago because he had *known* the rubies he had glimpsed in the display cabinet would look incredible against her luminous skin.

He had stood outside the exclusive establishment with the boxes in his pocket—once inside he had seen other items that had tempted him—when he had realised that he had just bought jewels worth a small fortune for a woman he never intended to see again.

Well, not intentionally see again—for a man not given to fantasizing, he had been spending a considerable amount of time imagining scenarios where they accidentally bumped into one another.

She would of course have realised in the interim that she had made a massive mistake and discovered that actually she could not live without him.

In the imagined scene he took her back, of course on his terms.

And as he stood there he recognised that there was a flaw in this scenario: the accidental part.

He was not a man who had ever left things to chance.

Why, he had asked himself, start now?

He had walked back to his office with a new sense of purpose—purpose that had been sadly lacking over the last few weeks.

He needed to work her out of his system. *Dios,* had he really been that stupid? Then he would regain the focus that had deserted him. He needed to tire of her because it was obvious that the woman and her damned eyes and the soft skin he woke up craving to touch were only still in his head because she had left him, she had walked.

Something no other woman had ever done, and she had done so before he had exhausted his interest in her.

Then he could move on.

It was rational to seek her out.

His self-delusion now seemed ridiculous in the extreme, but ridiculous or not it had lasted until last night when the truth had hit him with the force of a proverbial lightning bolt.

Why had he been afraid of admitting he loved her?

Maggie flushed at her own stupidity. She was seeing what she wanted to. He wasn't overcome with lust—he was just wondering what he had ever seen in a bag lady.

'Colour co-ordination wasn't high on my list of priorities this morning, and anyway,' she dismissed, 'you don't look so hot yourself.'

With a rueful expression Rafael ran a hand across his jaw. 'I would have asked your father to lend me a razor but he—'

'Has a beard,' she completed for him.

'And I don't think your brothers have started shaving yet.'

Maggie was distracted by the image of him in her home. 'You actually spent the night there?' She experienced a spasm of alarm as she noticed the greyish tinge to his normally vibrant skin. 'You obviously didn't get much sleep,' she observed concealing her anxiety behind a spiky attitude. 'You look worse than I do.'

CHAPTER SIXTEEN

MAGGIE stepped out of the lift from the garage and stopped, a small laugh drawn from her parted lips.

'Just how many houses do you have?' she asked, tilting her head back to look at the massive chandeliers suspended from the high ceiling. The wide sweeping staircase was perfect for making an impressive entrance. As she looked at it she could almost hear the swish of a silken skirt and feel the sensuous smoothness of the fabric on her bare skin.

'It's like a film set.' And I'm a character from another film, she thought, glancing down at her scuffed trainers that made no sound on the marble. Her jeans were a long way from the ball gown in her head and she was a long way from the sort of woman Rafael invited to host his London parties.

'What film did you have in mind?'

Maggie resisted the temptation to respond in a hushed tone—appropriate to this awe-inducing setting—and levelled a glare at his lean face, waiting until he had stopped speaking to a uniformed figure who had materialised before she narrowed her eyes and said, 'A film about someone with taste-less wealth, who kidnaps women!'

A flicker of impatience appeared in his eyes. 'This is not a kidnap—and we both know it—any more than it was the first time.'

Unable to bring herself to concede the truth of his edgy observation and feeling churlish because she supposed most people would acknowledge that he had actually rescued her, she pursed her lips and lowered her eyes.

'Myself, I always had a soft spot for misunderstood heroes.'

This comment brought her head up; her scornful scowl faded as she was hit by a badly timed debilitating surge of lust.

God, he was utterly gorgeous and his gorgeousness was not diminished by the dark shadow of stubble on his jaw or the exhaustion etched into his bronzed face.

The camera would love those strong angles and planes, and if it had been able to pick up even a fraction of the dark, smouldering, sexy aura he projected he would have been box office gold.

'Your problem is I do understand you,' she lied, thinking he had to be the most complex man on the planet; just when she thought she had figured him out he did something that totally threw her.

'But you think I am a hero—I'm flattered.'

'I might believe you if I didn't know you don't give a damn for anyone's opinion.' She stopped, wondering why they were wasting time on semantics.

She folded her arms over her chest and adopted a businesslike manner, always easier to do when your shaking hands were tucked safely out of view, and glanced at the doors leading off the hallway.

To her dazzled and slightly disorientated eyes there seemed to be dozens.

'So what next?' It was a question she hardly dared ask, let alone think about.

How did your life go back to any sort of normality after you had your face plastered all over the tabloids? How long in this situation did it take for the furore and speculation to die down…or maybe it never would?

Would she always be labelled the woman that a billionaire playboy gave a black eye?

On the brink of total panic she took a deep breath; all this speculation right now was pointless—what she needed to do was sort out one thing at a time.

Prioritising was not hard, and it was one of the few things in her life she still retained control of. She could at least concentrate on the positive: that she was not pregnant.

Struggling to capture that elusive positive frame of mind, she squeezed her eyelids closed, but the freeze-frame image that had formed in her head did not vanish.

For several moments she was forced to stare at Rafael gazing down proudly at the baby in his arms before she successfully banished it.

Dabbing the beads of sweat along her upper lip, she put a name to the tight, achy feeling in her chest: loss.

'Are you all right?'

Maggie's eyelashes lowered in a protective sweep. The sooner she cleared up the baby issue, the better, and how hard could it be to say there wasn't one?

He would probably break out the champagne.

He might even see the funny side of it, then again maybe not, she thought as she read the suspicion in his narrowed-eyed scrutiny.

Pasting on a smile brittle enough to break at the lightest touch or wrong word, she said brightly, 'I'm fine, it's just I think…'

Rafael, who had been watching the fluctuations of colour in her face, felt a stab of anxiety at the bluish discoloration of her lips. 'Are you going to faint?' He extended a hand that she patted irritably away.

Maggie breathed through a wave of nausea, tried to remember when she had last eaten and couldn't. Damn!

'I don't faint, just a blip. I'll be fine in a minute.'

'You are clearly not fine.' And it was his fault—everything was his fault.

Maggie lifted her head. 'Just a blood-sugar dip. I could just do with a cup of tea, that's all, and maybe a biscuit.'

Rafael was relieved to see that, though she was still pale, the blue discolouration around her lips had faded, but brave-face attitude did not fool him.

He studied her pale face, loving the curve of her cheek the tilt of her nose, her delicious mouth, loving even her stubbornness and fierce independence, but seeing past it to her fear.

She was holding it together, but only just. The need that rose up inside him, the need to remove the weight from her shoulders, to care for her, was totally outside his experience.

It was as strong in its own way as the wild, elemental attraction that existed between them. He was shaken to recognise it as part of the whole—it came with loving.

'Look, I know you must be scared. I know you must feel as if your life is over before it had begun.'

Maggie, confused by the intensity of his manner, looked startled and warily shook her head.

'But it doesn't have to be this way, Maggie. You may not believe it but if you could—'

He stopped abruptly and Maggie's level of bewilderment deepened as, in an utterly uncharacteristic action, his eyes slid from hers. He paused, the ripple of the muscles in his brown throat visible as he swallowed hard.

It was almost as if he were struggling to find the right words, which couldn't be right. Sure, Rafael was nobody's idea of chatty, and he never saw the need to fill a silence, but he was also extremely articulate.

As his head lifted the bands of colour along his cheekbones

drew Maggie's attention to the slashing contours. If this had been anyone else she would have said they were self-conscious—but this wasn't anyone else, it was Rafael, supremely confident Rafael, who she had never seen display anything approaching insecurity, even when he was stark naked. Palms damp with the effort, she pushed aside the erotic image of his lean, streamlined, golden-skinned body gleaming as shafts of moonlight hit... Focus, Maggie...

Moonlight and his body out of the equation one thing remained obvious: she was misreading the signs.

'One day you might look back and think this is the day your life, it began.'

She was startled not just by his words, but by the driven intensity of his manner and the emotion packed into his words. Her eyes lifted to his face and she saw the same intensity reflected in his smoky eyes as their glances locked.

'This is not something that you have to do alone.'

The husky resonance in his voice made her shiver. 'What do you mean?'

'I'm saying that I will not be an absent father. When we are married you will not have to worry about being a solo parent. I have much to learn,' he admitted.

The uncharacteristic display of humility passed right over Maggie's head. All she heard was *married...* He had said it so matter-of-factly that Maggie thought she had misheard.

'It's just as well I know your opinion of marriage, Rafael. For a moment there,' she admitted with a hollow little laugh, 'I thought you said *married.*'

Rafael did not share her mirth. 'A man can change his opinion.'

Maggie stared, drawn as always by the brooding strength in his face, but totally sure this was a case of crossed wires. Anything else was, well...*impossible!*

'You're suggesting we get married?' This time the laugh got locked in her aching throat.

His head reared back and he looked at her, hauteur and offence etched into every line of his dark patrician features. 'You thought I would not?'

Maggie blinked, realisation sending a soft pink wash over her skin.

He was serious.

This was a proposal. The fact he would hastily withdraw it did not alter the fact that he had made it.

Maggie admired the misplaced sense of honour that had made him propose, and even though she knew marriage under these circumstances was totally and utterly wrong she was unable to dispel the unsettling suspicion that, had she been carrying his baby, she could not have lived up to her own principles without a struggle.

She looked at him, a punch-drunk glaze in her wide eyes. 'I…I didn't think,' she admitted.

It looked to Rafael as if she wasn't thinking now; she looked as if adrenaline alone was keeping her upright. He grimaced and silently cursed the impatience that had made him prematurely blurt things out that way.

The priority was getting a medical all-clear because he still felt little confidence in the hospital's assurance she was fine.

In his view they were simply covering their backs against litigation. He would not relax until they had a diagnosis from a non-biased source.

'Wow, Rafael, I really appreciate the gesture, a really lovely gesture,' she began thickly. 'But you see—'

'You "appreciate"…!' he echoed.

'Yes, really, it's—'

'Yes.' He swallowed. 'You said—a *lovely* gesture.'

Maggie winced at the sardonic note in his voice.

'It is not a gesture, Maggie. We will speak of this afterwards.'

'No, I have to tell you now.'

Ignoring her anguished wail, Rafael walked over to a door and pushed it open. He turned and gestured for her to enter before him.

She sighed and, left with little choice, she acceded to the silent request and walked past him.

The room she found herself in appeared to be a large drawing room. It was not, however, the décor or antique furnishing that caught Maggie's attention, but the man standing next to the Adam fireplace.

'Maggie, this is Dr Metcalf…James,' he said, turning to the older man. 'I am grateful you came so promptly.'

Maggie watched the two men shake hands and felt her resentment stir. Did Rafael really think she would sit back and let him take control of her life this way? Maggie scowled and said loudly, 'I do not need a doctor.'

'Possibly,' Rafael conceded. 'But as he is here now it would be foolish, not to mention rude, to make this a wasted journey.'

Her jaw clenched. 'Don't patronise me, Rafael. If you want to waste your money on a totally unnecessary consultation that's your business, but I don't have to waste my time when I already know I'm fine.'

'So you are a doctor now.'

Maggie threw up her hands in utter exasperation. 'No, but I'm not a hypochondriac by proxy either.'

'Is that an accepted medical term?'

'Shut up, and in case,' she added coldly, 'you forgot, I was examined by a doctor after the incident.'

All humour evaporated from Rafael's manner as he scowled darkly. 'Not an incident,' he corrected. 'An assault, and not a doctor, a medical student.'

Maggie, who was not about to explain the intricacies of the

medical hierarchy, sighed. 'It doesn't take a Harley Street specialist to diagnose a black eye.'

Neither man denied the job description, but then this was no surprise. Rafael would only consult the best.

'For the record James—' his gaze was trained, not on the medic, but on Maggie '—and I explain because I understand that things such as uncharacteristic mood swings are sometimes diagnostic of an underlying problem with head injuries—but, no, she is always this unreasonable and difficult.'

Maggie's dark eyes flashed in response to this display of deliberate provocation. 'Thank you. I am in the room, and you are embarrassing the doctor.'

'Not at all,' the older man intervened smoothly. 'Now if you just give us a few minutes, Rafael, I'm sure I'll be able to put your fears to rest.'

Maggie rather enjoyed seeing the startled expression when Rafael realised he was being asked, albeit politely, to leave the room.

His steel-reinforced jaw tightened imperceptibly, but after a pause and what she suspected was a tough internal struggle—clearly his natural response to an order, even one couched as a polite suggestion, was not to smile—he nodded and produced one anyway.

Not that Maggie found the sardonic grin in her direction at all apologetic, but he did leave.

Maggie's shoulders sagged with relief when the door closed. It was a temporary reprieve, but at least it gave her breathing space and the opportunity to explain to the doctor that she really did not need a consultation.

The doctor agreed totally with her, which begged the question how did she end up being examined, anyway?

The examination was thorough but not lengthy. The doctor

pronounced that her facial injuries were superficial and advised she take painkillers to ease the discomfort.

Maggie said, 'I fine with pain, actually. It's just a bit uncomfortable.'

The doctor, who didn't look impressed by her stoicism, produced a bottle from his bag and handed it to her, saying, 'Just in case you change your mind and they won't harm the baby, but then you're a nurse—you already know that.'

Maggie's fingers tightened around the bottle as she managed to produce a half-hearted smile. She was not going to take her anger out on this man. She intended to reserve that for Rafael, who was a control freak of the first order.

Or maybe he wanted confirmation of the pregnancy? Ironic when if he'd only let her get a word in he'd already know there was no baby.

'I know Rafael is concerned that the attack could have harmed the baby…how far along are you?'

'There is no baby, doctor.'

CHAPTER SEVENTEEN

THE doctor had been gone a few minutes when, after a tap, the door opened. Maggie, who had been nursing her anger while she waited, spun around with a wrathful glower.

The maid holding the tea tray looked as startled as Maggie felt. She forced herself to smile and said thank you as the girl nervously put the tray down on a console table and beat a hasty retreat.

It was five minutes later when Rafael walked through the door, by which time Maggie had eaten several of the delicious smoked salmon and cream cheese sandwiches from the tray to revive her flagging energy levels and silence her growling stomach.

'How dare you go around telling people that I'm pregnant?'

'Shall I be mother or you?'

'Very funny.'

'I am not laughing,' he pointed out as he lowered his rangy frame onto a leather armchair.

A quick survey of his face through her lashes revealed that this was an accurate assessment; it was easy to read what he wasn't. What he was was more of a challenge and one beyond her capabilities.

'And I would not call one medic "people"—but as I was

asking him to examine you and make a diagnosis it seemed logical to give him all relevant medical information. And before you start accusing James of revealing confidential medical details, I can assure you the only information he imparted was that you are well.'

'But you tried?'

He flashed her an incredulous look as he crossed one ankle over the other and gritted, *'Dios,* you make me dizzy with your pacing. Sit before you fall down.' Rafael had to dig deep into his reserves of self restraint to stop himself leaping to his feet and physically enforcing his suggestion.

To see the pallor of sheer exhaustion etched into her delicate bruised face was a torment; not to respond to it intensified the agony.

'Of course I tried. It embarrassed me that I had to.'

Maggie winced as her sense of fair play kicked in hard. Shaking her hair back from her face, she lifted the stray strands that had crept down the neck of her top with her hand and flopped in an attitude of weary defeat into the chair opposite Rafael.

'All right, let's get this over with.'

'You make it sound like pulling a tooth.'

A procedure, she reflected grimly, that generally involved a local anaesthetic. This offered no such luxury. She expelled a shaky breath and watched as he left his seat to pour tea from the pot.

'Drink,' he said, handing her a cup before retaking his seat.

Maggie winced as she took a sip. 'I don't take sugar.'

'You look like you need it.'

'You're the one who will be in shock, not me.'

Rafael expelled a deep sigh and leaned forward, his hands planted on his knees.

'Susan's right—you are pregnant.' It emerged as a statement and not a question.

Maggie exhaled. 'No, I'm not,' she said, wondering whether he would be able to hide his relief.

There was no relief because it soon became clear he didn't believe a word she was saying. 'She is hurt you didn't feel able to tell her.'

'Of course I'd feel able to tell her—if I was. I'm just not.'

'She thought perhaps that you wanted to tell the baby's father first?'

'And you told her that was you...great, have you not been listening to me, Rafael? There is no baby!'

'Your mother is sure—'

'My mother has been sure that I'm pregnant ever since I got engaged to Simon.'

At the mention of the other man's name Rafael tensed.

'It was her worst fear. She never thought he was good for me—my entire family were relieved when we split up.' The same family that, it appeared, had welcomed Rafael with open arms.

One of life's little ironies.

Rafael's anger and frustration at her denial escalated.

'That won't wash. She didn't seem afraid to me—hurt because you hadn't told her and concerned because you bottle things up—'

He stopped as a hissing sound escaped through Maggie's clenched teeth.

'What's wrong?'

The question drew an incredulous laugh from Maggie. 'Why would anything be wrong?' she asked with bitter irony. 'My family has been discussing my character flaws with a stranger who walked in off the street!' she exploded.

'Not walked, exactly—I drove there.'

'Well, don't think you got preferential treatment because they were impressed with your big car. My family are not like that.'

'Yes, I did get that.' Having been born with a name that had been opening doors for him all his life, he had found it a strange experience to have a door stay firmly closed—until he had said the magic word: Maggie. 'I think they just liked me.'

'That's because she thought you were the father,' Maggie returned gloomily.

The smile that briefly lightened the brooding intensity of Rafael's expression had a definite hint of smugness. 'So you finally admit it.'

'No!' Maggie flicked a glance at his dark lean patrician profile and thought, She took one look at you and decided you were the catch of the century.

'I think Mum's mindset is almost anyone is better than Simon.'

It was name that he was fast growing to hate. 'If ever I need my ego deflated I will know where to come. This has nothing to do with...*Simon.* I am your first sexual relationship.' His glance drifted to her lips.

'But Mum doesn't know that, unless you told her?' Which was becoming a less ludicrous possibility by the second.

'It was not a subject that came up.'

'Well, thank God for that,' she breathed, thankful for small mercies.

'You are obviously very close. I assumed—'

'Can we leave my sex life out of this!' she cut in, not even making a pretence of being able to match his casual, almost careless attitude to that particular subject.

Meeting his eyes, she caught her breath and thought, Cancel careless. There was nothing that could be categorised careless in the glow reflected in those platinum depths.

'I have never discussed my sex life with Mum.'

'We will leave your sex life out of this, though I think it is very much part of it.'

He was struggling to be patient. He understood she was in denial, but her continued refusal to face up to facts was hard to take.

He had to make Maggie understand that he appreciated how she must be feeling and that he was going to be there for her—that she wasn't alone.

'I think Susan is a pragmatist. You are pregnant and, like any mother, she wants to know that you will be looked after.'

Maggie lifted her hands in a gesture of utter frustration.

'And,' he said, ignoring the interruption, 'I reassured her on the subject.'

'Oh, God!' Maggie groaned, lifting her knees to her chest and wrapping her arms around them. 'I'm not pregnant!'

A hissing sound of anger escaped through his clenched teeth. 'Will you stop pretending, Maggie? I saw the baby clothes.'

She watched in bemused silence as he got to his feet and stalked to the opposite end of the room with the grace of a restless caged panther. He was so damned gorgeous that even the sight of his broad back made her ache.

The swell of longing that tightened in her chest made it hard for Maggie to speak as she echoed.

'"Baby clothes"?'

He spun back, dragging a hand over his dark hair as he pinned her with a lethal steely glare of disapproval. 'Isn't it about time you stopped this act?'

'I'm not acting.'

Her response did not soften the grim severity of his expression. 'In the bathroom, the boxes.' He saw the realisation wash across her face and said, 'Finally! Now can we start discussing this like two adults?'

Maggie covered her mouth with her hand. 'You saw the clothes and thought…' She stopped, exhaled a shaky sigh. 'So that was why you left so suddenly?' It was totally illogical of her to feel hurt by the fact he had been so spooked that his first instinct had been to run.

The fact was he had come back, even though a baby was the last thing he wanted in his life, because despite his reputation Rafael was a thoroughly decent man, and with a strong sense of responsibility.

And because he was a decent man he would try to hide his relief when he realised the truth, she thought bleakly.

'I'm not pregnant, Rafael. No!' She held up her hand and said quickly, 'Please, just hear me out.' She paused, choosing her words with care, ashamed that for a split second she had wished there had been a baby and she would have an excuse to keep him in her life.

'There were baby clothes in the boxes. A friend at work passed them on to me because she knew—'

'That you are pregnant.'

'No, she knew about the work I do at the shelter.'

His dark brows twitched into a frowning line above his hawkish nose. '"Shelter"?' Was this yet another diversion?

'When Simon was campaigning during the by-election he visited a shelter. It's a place,' she explained, 'where women who are escaping abusive relationships go. They stay there while they get back on their feet. Some have children with them.'

Simon, happy with the results of the photo opportunity, had seen no reason to go back, privately confiding that he had found the entire experience depressing.

When asked if she felt the same way Maggie had admitted she had been shocked but not depressed; actually she had found her visit to the shelter, if anything, uplifting.

The people who worked there, she had explained to him, had been so tremendously dedicated, and the courage and resilience of many of the women who, despite all they had been through, were looking forward to starting a new life inspirational.

Simon had been unable to understand her attitude and he had been less than happy when she had continued the association with the shelter, not on any formal basis, but she had become quite involved with fundraising.

'Some of the women have children and babies.'

He leaned his broad shoulders against the wall and studied her face in silence for what felt like an eternity to Maggie.

'This is true?'

She nodded.

'And the clothes, they are for them?'

She nodded again.

'How do you have time for this shelter? You work impossible hours and—'

'So do you.'

'That is not the same...' He exhaled slowly and met her eyes. 'So you are not pregnant,' he said, not portraying any particular relief, but then maybe it was still sinking in.

'No, so you can relax—you're not going to be a father.' It was difficult not to notice that he didn't look relaxed.

Rafael passed a hand across his eyes and peeled himself away from the wall. His demeanour as he walked across the room toward her was not one she would have associated with a man who had just had a narrow escape.

As he got closer Maggie's levels of nervous tension soared. There was something ominous about his body language and she began to talk, the words tripping over each other in her nervous haste to get them out.

'I'm sorry you had all the worry and my mum made it worse. Some men would have walked away.'

He stopped a few feet from her. 'I did.' In shock or not it was a response that he would never forgive himself for. 'I was a coward.' He had not known how to tell her he loved her.

'A bit harsh.'

He gave her a long level look. 'Not harsh enough.'

The depth of self-condemnation in his voice made her blink.

'You did come back and it's all a happy ending. No baby, no wedding bells.'

Rafael continued to stare back at her, not looking like a man who was celebrating his lucky escape.

Maggie's control snapped. She didn't need this. It was tough enough putting a cheerful face on the fact that there was nothing beyond a physical attraction which by his own estimation only had a short time to run before it fizzled out—at least on his part—to keep them together.

Rafael was going to walk away some time soon and this time he wouldn't come back, and he was standing there acting as if it were his life that had just fallen apart.

'It doesn't change anything.'

Maggie was startled by this incomprehensible interpretation of the situation.

'It changes everything, Rafael. You came here to ask me to be your mistress, not your wife.'

His upper lip curled in an expression of contempt and he reviewed his behaviour. He took her chin in his fingers and with his free hand brushed the strands of dark hair from her face. The tenderness in the action brought a rush of tears to her eyes. 'I spent a long time trying to work out why I came here, but last night I realised it is not complicated.'

'It isn't?' Maggie whispered. The tender glow in his magnificent eyes was sending all sorts of messages that she didn't dare believe.

'The answer is just as simple as when you asked me earlier did I have to kiss you.' A distracted expression appeared in his smoky eyes as his thumb moved along the curve of her soft lush lips. 'I *had* to come to you.'

The throaty admission was good, but suddenly Maggie wanted more—she dared to think that there was more. 'Why?'

'I do not function without you in my life. It was a shock to learn you were pregnant, or I thought you were,' he corrected, flashing her a bitter grin.

'Look, you were allowed to be unhappy. No man wants to be saddled with a baby from a casual fling.'

'Is that what we were?'

Her eyes fell, she swallowed…was it possible…? She could not let herself believe. She felt his hands on her shoulders and lifted her face to his. The incandescent glow in his eyes made her gasp.

'It was never a simple fling for me, Maggie,' he said quietly. 'I told myself it was but that was just a front because I didn't have the guts to admit the truth.' He shook his head in disgust.

'And what is that?'

'The truth is I stopped refusing to admit the truth about us. And, for the record, once the initial shock wore off I was delighted about the baby, and not just because it bound you to me.'

Maggie shook her spinning head, unable to take in what he was saying. 'What are you saying? You want me to be your mistress?'

'Mistress?' He took her face between his hands and gazed down into her eyes with an expression that brought tears of emotion to them. 'No! I want you to be my wife.'

'Marry…me…you…'

'That,' he said lovingly, 'is the general idea.' He fitted his warm lips to the quivering outline of her mouth and kissed her until she was breathless. 'I love you,' he breathed against her mouth. 'And I have been lost without you.'

'This is real.' She pressed a hand to her mouth, but was obliged to remove it when he kissed her again. 'You love me?'

Finally allowing herself to believe that this really was happening, Maggie let out a euphoric whoop of joy and flung her arms around his neck.

'And I love you, I adore you...' she declared, punctuating each word with a kiss. Breathless she lifted a loving hand to his face. 'You do know, don't you, that I would do anything for you?' she husked emotionally.

'This is good to know, but I discovered that my needs are actually quite simple, *mi querida.*'

'They are?'

He took the hand laid against his face, holding her eyes with his as he pressed her palm to his lips. The heat in his eyes made her insides tighten. 'Yes. It turns out after a life of driven achievement, all I actually need is you.'

She blinked away the tears of happiness that filled her eyes. 'Are you saying I'm simple?'

'I'm saying that you are infuriating, stubborn, argumentative!' Stilling her protest with a brush of his lips that made her tremble, he added huskily, 'And I wouldn't want you any other way. Without you I'm not even sure I exist, Maggie. If that makes sense.'

Maggie nodded. 'It does to me, and if that is the case then I think I'd better stay for more than a week this time.'

'A lifetime would not be long enough for me to show you all the ways I love you.'

She laughed up into his dark beautiful face and said solemnly, 'Then as time is an issue maybe you should start now—showing me, that is...'

It was an invitation that Rafael found he had no problem accepting.

'Out of curiosity,' he added as he lifted her into his arms and looked with love into her eyes. *'Dio!'* he groaned, distracted by the love glowing back at him. 'You are beautiful.' After a pause for a kiss that left her aching for more he added,

'I know your feelings on shoes, but what is your attitude on jewellery? I like the idea of rubies on your skin.'

Maggie who liked the idea of *Rafael* on her skin nodded happily. 'Anything you say.'

'No arguments?'

'Me?' she said innocently then laughed huskily when he rolled his eyes. 'I concede that it is just possible I might occasionally disagree with you. But if all our arguments end this way I have no complaints!'

'I think I find that I believe in happy endings.'

'Surely not,' she teased as he strode from the room.

'I must—I have found mine. Now we will begin the tour of the house. Starting, I think, in the master bedroom, which you might like to redecorate.'

Maggie linked her arms around his neck. 'I wouldn't change a thing.'

Why change perfection?

EPILOGUE

THE doting grandmothers had been reluctant to relinquish their burden, but Rafael remained firm as he took possession of the irritable baby.

And no wonder he was irritable, Rafael thought, able to identify with his son's demeanour.

Left to him this would have been a small intimate celebration with guests whom you could tell to go home at the appropriate moment without causing outrage. This was *definitely* the last time he would open his home to his family.

Until the next time Maggie smiled and said, *'Please, Rafael,'* he thought with a wry grin.

His focus shifted to the other side of the room where his wife, looking totally drop-dead gorgeous in a striking red dress and oblivious as always to the fact half the men in the room were lusting after her, was doing her perfect hostess thing.

When people asked, as they always did, if he knew how lucky he was, Rafael was able to honestly say—yes.

The conversation with Rafael's elderly aunt was stretching Maggie's novice Spanish to the limit. It was Angelina who rescued her.

'Thanks for that.'

Angelina smiled. 'You looked as if you were struggling. Oh, not again,' she sighed, turning at the sound of a cry.

Maggie watched amused as Angelina ran gracefully across the room to pick up her sobbing toddler from the floor. Her twin half brothers had reached the terrible two stage.

Only a second behind her Susan Ward was on the spot, bending to lift the remaining twin into her arms, a handful of his brother's hair still clutched triumphantly in his chubby fist.

They had had a noisy and very happy family party when Mum's operation had been officially declared a total success.

Maggie watched as the two women—her *mothers*—their heads close together, laughed. The previous night Maggie had found herself taking snaps of her mum teaching Angelina the dance she had learnt at her salsa class!

Now how weird was that? she thought. Only it wasn't. The first few times she'd met up with Angelina had been strained, but over time they had become quite close. Not in a mother-daughter way—they were too close in age for that—but they had become friends and Angelina had really helped her settle into her new life, not to mention persuading Rafael not to wrap her up in cotton wool during her pregnancy.

Maggie hadn't asked about her natural father, and she knew the other woman was grateful she had left this painful subject alone.

Maggie feared that being outed as illegitimate might have made her some sort of social outcast, but she had been wrong. There had of course been gossip, but far from being an outcast she had been embraced by both Spanish clans, who seemed anxious to claim her as their own.

Angelina's reaction to having her secret made public had surprised Maggie. It was a relief, she insisted, to finally have everything out in the open, and though Maggie had no idea what had gone on behind closed doors Alfonso certainly appeared to have totally accepted the situation.

Maggie reached Rafael's side just as he was tucking their son expertly against his shoulder. An emotional lump swelled in her throat as she watched him supporting their son's small head tenderly with one big hand.

Though she teased Rafael about his protective attitude to their son, she totally understood it. Alessandro had been so tiny and fragile when he was born that she had been almost too scared to touch him, but he was catching up fast.

She lifted a hand and stroked his silky head. They called him their 'wedding-night baby' because he had been due nine months to the day following their wedding. Alessandro had, however, decided to do his own thing and arrive six weeks early.

Maggie had spent that first couple of weeks when he was being monitored in the special care baby unit in a state of constant anxiety. If it hadn't been for Rafael, who had been incredible supporting her through that scary time, Maggie wasn't sure she could have coped.

His dark lashes curled from his flushed cheek and Maggie smiled as their perfect beautiful baby boy looked directly at her.

'He looks more like you every day.'

'Is that a good thing?' Rafael asked with a teasing smile.

'Ask me the same question in eighteen years' time when he is breaking hearts and if he's like his papa, rules, too.' She smiled, cheerful when considering this moment that was still safely distant.

'Sixteen,' Rafael corrected. 'We Castenadas are early developers.' The baby in his arms chose that moment to give a loud cry. 'He needs a nap. I'll take him to the nursery.'

'I'll do it if you like?' she offered.

Rafael shook his head, meeting her eyes above the soft froth of baby curls. 'I need a break from our guests.' The scowling glance he threw around the room drew a laugh from Maggie. 'Shouldn't they be going?'

'Play nice, Rafael. Remember we did them out of a wedding,' she reminded him.

Rafael, it turned out was not a fan of long engagements. Theirs had lasted only as long as it took to push through the legalities before she had walked the hundred yards to the church from her parents' house.

The only guests present had been her parents and brothers and she and Rafael had spent the next month in a villa owned by Rafael's Greek billionaire friend Theo Leonidis.

'I think we owe them today.'

'Owe them!' he ejaculated, shaking his head before adding, 'How you ever persuaded me to say yes to this!'

Maggie feigned innocence and angled a wide-eyed look at his face. 'You don't remember?'

Rafael's eyes darkened as they slid to her wide lush lips. 'You can remind me later.'

Their eyes connected and a familiar bolt of lust slammed through her body. 'A date,' she agreed huskily, laying a hand on his arm and raising herself up on tiptoe to kiss her son's forehead. 'Yell if you need me.'

'I always need you.' His eyes travelled from the baby in his arms to the face of the woman he loved, loved with such an intensity that it still took his breath away just to see her smile. He suspected it always would.

Maggie tilted her head to one side, a wicked smile playing over her lips as she said huskily, 'Our guests don't seem to want to leave, but there's nothing stopping us, is there? They probably won't even notice,' she predicted.

Rafael a gleam in his eyes, nodded. 'I like your thinking, Magdalena,' he said admiringly.

Maggie grinned and slanted a sultry look up at him through her dark lashes. 'Is there anything else you like?'

'It depends on what's on offer.'

She lifted herself on tiptoe, this time to whisper a suggestion in his ear. Rafael raised his brows and grinned.

'I could be persuaded,' he admitted, sliding his free arm around her waist as he headed for the open door.

'I think he's asleep,' Maggie whispered.

'Of course he's asleep—his timing is as good as his father's.'

'Says you!' Maggie teased.

'No,' he contradicted smoothly. 'Says you...often. Have I ever mentioned that you turned my world upside down?'

'Only once or twice a day.'

'You know,' he mused, his glance sliding from the flushed face of his sleeping son to the glowing beauty of his wife's upturned features, 'I don't know if I'm standing on my head or my heels, but I love the view from here.'

'It's not bad from where I'm standing either,' Maggie returned, her loving gaze glued to the face of the tall Spaniard who had captured her heart. 'Sometimes,' she confessed, 'I think this is a dream and I'll wake up and all this will be gone.'

Rafael bent his head and kissed her tenderly. 'When you wake up I will be there, *mi querida.* Now come, before our guests spot us and decide to follow us to our bedroom.'

Maggie gave a sigh of contentment. 'God, but I love being irresistible!'

'And I love you.'

JUNE 2010 HARDBACK TITLES

ROMANCE

Marriage: To Claim His Twins	Penny Jordan
The Royal Baby Revelation	Sharon Kendrick
Under the Spaniard's Lock and Key	Kim Lawrence
Sweet Surrender with the Millionaire	Helen Brooks
The Virgin's Proposition	Anne McAllister
Scandal: His Majesty's Love-Child	Annie West
Bride in a Gilded Cage	Abby Green
Innocent in the Italian's Possession	Janette Kenny
The Master of Highbridge Manor	Susanne James
The Power of the Legendary Greek	Catherine George
Miracle for the Girl Next Door	Rebecca Winters
Mother of the Bride	Caroline Anderson
What's A Housekeeper To Do?	Jennie Adams
Tipping the Waitress with Diamonds	Nina Harrington
Saving Cinderella!	Myrna Mackenzie
Their Newborn Gift	Nikki Logan
The Midwife and the Millionaire	Fiona McArthur
Knight on the Children's Ward	Carol Marinelli

HISTORICAL

Rake Beyond Redemption	Anne O'Brien
A Thoroughly Compromised Lady	Bronwyn Scott
In the Master's Bed	Blythe Gifford

MEDICAL™

From Single Mum to Lady	Judy Campbell
Children's Doctor, Shy Nurse	Molly Evans
Hawaiian Sunset, Dream Proposal	Joanna Neil
Rescued: Mother and Baby	Anne Fraser

JUNE 2010 LARGE PRINT TITLES

ROMANCE

The Wealthy Greek's Contract Wife	Penny Jordan
The Innocent's Surrender	Sara Craven
Castellano's Mistress of Revenge	Melanie Milburne
The Italian's One-Night Love-Child	Cathy Williams
Cinderella on His Doorstep	Rebecca Winters
Accidentally Expecting!	Lucy Gordon
Lights, Camera…Kiss the Boss	Nikki Logan
Australian Boss: Diamond Ring	Jennie Adams

HISTORICAL

The Rogue's Disgraced Lady	Carole Mortimer
A Marriageable Miss	Dorothy Elbury
Wicked Rake, Defiant Mistress	Ann Lethbridge

MEDICAL™

Snowbound: Miracle Marriage	Sarah Morgan
Christmas Eve: Doorstep Delivery	Sarah Morgan
Hot-Shot Doc, Christmas Bride	Joanna Neil
Christmas at Rivercut Manor	Gill Sanderson
Falling for the Playboy Millionaire	Kate Hardy
The Surgeon's New-Year Wedding Wish	Laura Iding

MILLS & BOON®

JULY 2010 HARDBACK TITLES

ROMANCE

A Night, A Secret...A Child	Miranda Lee
His Untamed Innocent	Sara Craven
The Greek's Pregnant Lover	Lucy Monroe
The Mélendez Forgotten Marriage	Melanie Milburne
Sensible Housekeeper, Scandalously Pregnant	Jennie Lucas
The Bride's Awakening	Kate Hewitt
The Devil's Heart	Lynn Raye Harris
The Good Greek Wife?	Kate Walker
Propositioned by the Billionaire	Lucy King
Unbuttoned by Her Maverick Boss	Natalie Anderson
Australia's Most Eligible Bachelor	Margaret Way
The Bridesmaid's Secret	Fiona Harper
Cinderella: Hired by the Prince	Marion Lennox
The Sheikh's Destiny	Melissa James
Vegas Pregnancy Surprise	Shirley Jump
The Lionhearted Cowboy Returns	Patricia Thayer
Dare She Date the Dreamy Doc?	Sarah Morgan
Neurosurgeon . . . and Mum!	Kate Hardy

HISTORICAL

Vicar's Daughter to Viscount's Lady	Louise Allen
Chivalrous Rake, Scandalous Lady	Mary Brendan
The Lord's Forced Bride	Anne Herries

MEDICAL™

Dr Drop-Dead Gorgeous	Emily Forbes
Her Brooding Italian Surgeon	Fiona Lowe
A Father for Baby Rose	Margaret Barker
Wedding in Darling Downs	Leah Martyn

MILLS & BOON®

JULY 2010 LARGE PRINT TITLES

ROMANCE

Greek Tycoon, Inexperienced Mistress	Lynne Graham
The Master's Mistress	Carole Mortimer
The Andreou Marriage Arrangement	Helen Bianchin
Untamed Italian, Blackmailed Innocent	Jacqueline Baird
Outback Bachelor	Margaret Way
The Cattleman's Adopted Family	Barbara Hannay
Oh-So-Sensible Secretary	Jessica Hart
Housekeeper's Happy-Ever-After	Fiona Harper

HISTORICAL

One Unashamed Night	Sophia James
The Captain's Mysterious Lady	Mary Nichols
The Major and the Pickpocket	Lucy Ashford

MEDICAL™

Posh Doc, Society Wedding	Joanna Neil
The Doctor's Rebel Knight	Melanie Milburne
A Mother for the Italian's Twins	Margaret McDonagh
Their Baby Surprise	Jennifer Taylor
New Boss, New-Year Bride	Lucy Clark
Greek Doctor Claims His Bride	Margaret Barker